IS INDIA READY FOR A LONG WAR?

NIL

COL (RETD) BHASKAR SARKAR VSM

DEDICATION

This book is dedicated to the Indians who agree with Lord Chetwode's moto:

"The safety, honour and welfare of my country comes first always and every time!

The safety, honour and welfare of my men come next!

My own safety, honour and welfare comes last, always and every time!"

Contents

Prologue

Prologue

"The art of war teaches us not to rely on the likelihood of the enemy not coming, but on our readiness to receive him: not on the chance of his not attacking but rather on the fact that we have made our position unassailable."

- Sun Tzu, Chinese scholar, and military strategists in 500 BC

India is a soft state. Our patriotism is limited to dying for the country. **We do** not believe in preparing for winning wars. When Mohammad Ghori used to attack the Somnath Temple of Gujrat, thousands of Indians rushed to battle with whatever weapons they could muster and were massacred by Mohammad's well trained and well-equipped forces. The invaders went away with gold, jewellery, and women. They kept returning year after year and sacked the Somnath Temple no less than thirteen times without effective resistance. Prithvi Raj Chauhan defeated, and captured Mohammad Ghori and let him go. Next year Prithvi Raj Chauhan, betrayed by father-in-law Jai Chand, was defeated at the battle of Terrain, captured by Ghori, and taken to Kabul, blinded, and later executed.

Things have not changed. We suffered a humiliating defeat in the war with China in 1962. General Henderson Brook's report on the causes of defeat is still not public after 62 years. The lesson from that war, and other wars India has fought since independence have been forgotten and the manpower situation is quite similar to that before the Chinese attacks in 1962. We fought four wars with Pakistan and won one in 1971. That victory was possible because Mrs. Indira Gandhi modernized the Indian Army with Soviet weapons and General Manekshaw could persuade Mrs. Gandhi to delay the operations till the preparations were complete. It was also due to the outstanding strategic and tactical abilities of General Manekshaw, General Arora and General Sagat Singh and outstanding valour and leadership displayed by the young officers. We ran out of ammunition for Bofors guns during the 30-day Kargil war. Large numbers of air force pilots die in peace time training due to old aircraft and poor maintenance. Politicians, people, men, and media eulogize the sacrifices of the armed forces. Awards and grants of lands, petrol pumps are announced after wars though not always released. Then everyone forgets the lessons of the war.

It is business as usual. I fear that military leadership and operational readiness are at pre-1962 levels. The private sector, intelligentsia and electronic media criticize the size of the defence budget. The armed forces and their requirements for modernization and being battle ready are put on the back burner. Knee jerk procurements cannot substitute the need for sustained indigenous developments and production like China. Budget allocation for modernization remains unspent every year due to bureaucratic bungling. Does anyone know the real state of readiness of our combat units? Bragging about our defence capability and half truths about modernization bandied about by media creates a sense of complacency. No one cares. Service Chiefs never complain lest their post-retirement benefits are endangered.

Our political leaders and administrators have an ostrich mentality. Pandit Nehru was either so gullible that he saw no danger in the induction of Chinese Army into Tibet or found it expedient to ignore it. Our government became aware of Chinese incursions only after the Chinese had annexed Aksai Chin. We paid no attention to modernizing our defence forces till after the 1962 debacle. We fought the state of art American Patton tanks of the Pakistan Army during 1965 War with Second World War Sherman and Centurion tanks. The Sherman tank shells used to bounce off the Patton tanks and could cause no damage. We survived the war without major losses by some good fortune and inept strategic and tactical ability of the Pakistani Generals. MIG 29 have been phased out by Russia but are front line fighters of the Indian Air Force. One squadron of Rafale fighters have been purchased from France but there is no public information about whether the second part of the deal, assembly in India, is being done in India. There is no news whether Tejas MK I fighters are being produced in large numbers and whether the MK II version has been introduced into service and what is production capability.

The armed forces have been relegated to the fringes of power and play second fiddle to the politicians, bureaucrats and even police officers. Essential equipment and spares are not procured in time. Pliable officers are promoted to positions of authority. Vacancies of more than 8,000 junior officers and 100,000 soldiers weaken the Army. Regular recruitment has stopped. To cap it all, we have 'Agnieers," four-year contract soldiers to defend us in future wars, because government is unwilling to pay pensions.

The future of our country depends not only on our economic policies but also on our defence and foreign policies. These in turn depend on the attitude, ability and acumen of our political leaders, security advisers, intellectuals, and media to read the military capabilities and intentions of our neighbours. Capabilities take time to build. Intensions can change overnight as we have seen in recent regime change in Bangladesh.

Technology has entered warfare in a big way. Remotely controlled missiles and drones are causing unprecedented level of destruction and casualties wherever they have been used. Are defence against these new threats available to us in the required quantities? It should also be noted that technology has not reduced the requirement of well trained and motivated boots on the ground.

1962 found the nation unprepared to meet the Chinese aggression. The officer and manpower state has fallen to pre-1962 levels. Unless we become aware of Chinese Armed Forces organizations, modernization, weapon systems and strategies and acquire ability to neutralize them, we will be found wanting when the time comes in the same way as we were found wanting in 1962.

It is well known that the Chinese have encircled India over the last fifty years by buying influence in Pakistan, Nepal, Myanmar, Bangladesh, Sri Lanka, and Maldives. The comparative weakness of the Indian Armed Forces vis a vis what China and its allies can deploy against us if it chooses to is well known to our armed forces and political leaders. The regime change in Bangladesh poses a very serious threat to India's security.

The aim of this book is to force our political and military leaders to examine the state of our defence preparedness and take positive actions before it becomes too late. **Since important people have little time to read, each chapter ends with a summary and an analysis.**

The aim of this book is not to criticize any individual. It aims to highlight the weaknesses in our attitude, institutions, policies, priorities, out dated British era traditions and practices of our government departments and the armed forces and suggest changes and solutions to problems. Our beloved Prime Minister has revised the British Era laws. Would he kindly order review, improvement, and eradication of British Era inefficient practices that plague the government agencies and armed forces and introduce cost effective ones without compromising national security.

I hope it is not a crime to disagree with Adam Smith's neoliberal economic thought of minimum government and maximum profit motive being always beneficial for a country. I believe in the Keynesian economic model where the governments control destinies of countries and its people and not profit motive of our million millionaires and billionaires. I do not believe that India can become a developed nation unless all Indians are disciplined, educated, healthy and learn to live in harmony with the diverse religious and cultural heritage of our great nation.

President Trump says "America First" and most Americans cheer. Long time back Lord Chetwood had inscribed at the Indian Military Academy in Dehradun; "The honour and welfare of my country comes first always and every time, the honour and welfare of my men come next; my own honour and welfare comes last always and every time." If only our political and military leaders could remember and follow this ideal. If they could, India would be strong, and "heaven on earth".

It is not out of place to mention that all information connected to military strengths of countries, economic data etc. are based either the Internet and published books. No access to classified information has been has been made.

I would like to emphasize that my comments are not directed at any person or political party but made in good faith and for the good of our great nation.

Col Bhaskar Sarkar

colbhaskarvsm@gmail.com

Contents

CHAPTER ONE

Geopolitical Situation April 2025

The entire world seems to be at war. However, Ukraine War and China's territorial claims including over South China Sea has polarized the world as never before. There are two main groups. On one side we have NATO, Israel, Ukraine, South Korea, Japan, and Taiwan. On the other side is Russia, China, North Korea, Pakistan, Iran, and its axis of resistance including Houthis and Hezbollah.

India is with both sides. It is a part of the US led QUAD and an active supporter of the Israeli war machine. Its Navy has played an effective role in curbing piracy off Somalia and in the Arabian Sea. India is also a friend of Russia and Iran. Russia has been India's primary arms supplier from late sixties till the Vajpayee regime. It is also providing with the S400 air defence system. However, the number of systems being provided by different countries and what these systems can protect is not very clear. Iran and Russia have provided crude oil to India and India is executing some vital infrastructure projects in Iran. In the face of new US sanctions on Iran it is not clear if the relationship will continue. Russia has also formed what it calls the Afghan QUAD. It consists of Russia, China, Pakistan, and Iran. Russia has invited India to join the group. It is highly unlikely that India will unless its relationship with the US sours. It well could if the US repatriates all illegal Indian immigrants in the US and imposes 100% or reciprocal tariff on imports from India. India has agreed to repatriate illegal immigrants from the US to placate Trump. But will that satisfy the US President? As of 2022, over 750,000 un-documented Indian immigrants are in the US. Another 170,000 have been detained by the US immigration while attempting to illegally enter the US. (**Source: "Why Indians are risking all to chase their American Dream", by Soutik Biswas, BBC, 25**

Nov, 2024.) Illegal immigrants are a large source of foreign exchange remittance. If India is forced to repatriate the entire 920,000 illegal immigrants, there will be chaos and loss of billions of dollars of foreign exchange remittances. It will severely affect India's current account deficit and lead to further devaluation of the Indian Rupee.

In case the Ukraine War or battle for the South China Sea and Taiwan leads to the Third World War, India will try to remain neutral but is likely to go with the US. In case of a conflict with China, Russia will possibly side with China and India may be forced to seek the help of the US and Israel.

The new US President, Donald Trump has promised to prevent a Third World War. He had also said that he would end the Ukraine War in 24 hrs. That has not happened. The War in Ukraine has intensified with Ukraine using long range missiles and drones to attack Russian defence production units and energy infrastructure deep inside Russian territory. Russia is already retaliating and the War is likely to escalate and may well lead to World War III.

President Trump has said that Putin is destroying Russia. (**Source: Global Times, Times of India, Chennai edition, Jan 22, 2025**) That is not a sign of bonhomie. The statement and Trump's tirade against BRICKS has made Russia and China ties even stronger. It is a question of survival for the two nations. Hence, cold war between the two will only intensify. But they are going to meet in Saudi Arabia soon. The outcome of the meeting will have significant global implications. India is a part of QUAD which is a part of an US led naval force directed against China. How long India can "run with the hares and hunt with the hounds" will be interesting to see.

Trump's "America First Policy" and insistence on only use of the US Dollar in international trade could complicate things for India and force it to choose sides. Trump is against BRICKS alliance of which India is a founding member and has warned of imposing 100% tariff on imports from BRICKS nations. The US is the only trading partner with which India has a trade surplus. Disruption of trade with the US will hurt India badly.

The US has offered to supply India with its latest air defence systems or stealth aircraft. But no decision has been made by India that is in public domain. India will at best be a source of boots on ground for the US or Russia and a large market for the US, especially armaments, oil and motor cycles. Russia could also pressurize China to avoid a major conflict with India. India's dependence on crude oil imports will ensure it remains vulnerable to US sanctions and a war in the Arabian Peninsula.

The US President, Donald Trump has pulled the US out of treaty obligation like Paris Climate Change agreement and international organizations like World Health Organization on the first day in office. It signals the end to the world order established after World War II with the establishment of the United Nations and various international organizations. His threats of taking Panama Canal and Greenland by force signals a return to the medieval concept of "might is right and justice is but the luxury of fools." He has also said that the US will take over Gaza, remove Palestinians and transform Gaza into a riviera. It gives green-light to China to take over Taiwan, South China Sea and all disputed territories including Arunachal by force. It gives green light to Israel to annexe Palestinian territories and even Lebanon with the US's consent. India and all nations have but one option; become a vassal of the US or join forces opposed to its hegemony. Time will tell what India will do.

President Trump has asked President Putin to end the war in Ukraine by making a deal with President Zelensky. He has threatened to impose severe sanction on Russia if it does not do so. President Putin has said that he is ready for discussions but President Zelensky is not. The Russian President is also unlikely to give up his three main demands; Donbass must be recognized as Russian territory; Ukraine will not be a member of NATO and the strength of Ukraine's armed forces must not exceed 50,000. None of these conditions are acceptable to President Zelensky. In fact, he has escalated drone and missile attacks deep inside Russia and caused considerable damage. The US has suspended all foreign aid for a period of 90 days. This means that Ukraine will not receive any aid for the next three months. This appears to be an attempt by Trump to force President Zelensky to the negotiating table. Ukraine's reactions are awaited. The suspension of aid may also be suspended or paused as are the duties on Canadian and Mexican exports to the US.

President Trump has also asked Saudi Arabia and OPEC to bring down oil. prices by producing more. His aim is to hurt Russia economically and force Russia to stop the war. If Saudi Arabia and OPEC did try, Russia could persuade Iran, who will also be hurt by reduced oil prices, to close the Strait of Hormuz and get Houthi's to attack oil production and storage facilities in Saudi Arabia, Kuwait, and Qatar. That would send oil prices through the roof and hurt EU very badly.

Another very significant development which affects India is the regime change in Bangladesh. With Sheikh Hasina and Awami League overthrown,

Bangladesh has become hostile to India and friendly with Pakistan and China. This factor will be discussed in Chapter 4: Threat from Bangladesh.

The Pahalgam terrorist massacre has brought things to boil. It has brought India and Pakistan close to war. India has promised to end cross border terrorism. Its diplomatic and economic offensive is well known to all. The suspense is with regard to what military action it takes. The Indian media is agog with praise for the invincible Indian Armed Forces. I not sure whether the hype is justified. I hope India will act only when it is fully ready as it did in 1971.

Summary

The entire world seems to be at war. Ukraine War and a conflict in South China Sea has the potential to lead to World War III.

The world is divided into two groups with many fence sitters. The primary one, led by the US has NATO, Japan, South Korea, Taiwan, and Australia. The competing one has Russia, China, Iran, Pakistan, and North Korea. The rest of the countries sitting on the fence lean in different directions. India is doing its best to be friendly to both sides.

There are two QUADs. First consists of the US, Japan, Australia, and India. It is mainly active in the South China Sea and Indian Ocean. The second QUAD named the Afghan QUAD has Russia, China, Iran, and Pakistan. The main aim is to counter the other QUAD.

Donald Trump's victory in the US Presidential elections has thrown the world into a turmoil. His "America First" and anti-immigrant and anti-UN policies have thrown the world into great uncertainty. His flaunting the US military power, utter disregard for UN and international law, and expansionist threats of annexing Greenland, Panama Canal and Gaza by force could encourage China to do the same.

The political unrest in Bangla Desh which led to the ouster of Sheikh Hasina and her Awami League government poses a serious threat to India's security.

The Pahalgam terrorist massacre has brought India and Pakistan close to war. India has promised to end cross border terrorism. The suspense is with regard to what military action it takes. I hope India will act only when it is fully ready as it did in 1971.

Analysis

It is important that India does not take sides and reviews it economic and defence strategies keeping that of the US in mind, and according to the current geopolitical situation.

India must consider its military options with due diligence keeping in mind the military aid that is coming to Pakistan from Turkey and China, a hostile Bangladesh and its own state of readiness.

India must immediately start preparing for a long war and disruption of crude oil supplies.

Threat From Pakistan

History of Hostilities 1947-2000

Hostilities between Pakistan and India started immediately after independence. It was over Jammu and Kashmir state joining India. Kashmir was a Muslim majority state with a Hindu king. Hence, Pakistan wanted it to be a part of Pakistan. It attacked India in September 1947 by sending irregular raiders. When the raiders were stopped by the Indian army just west of Srinagar, the Pakistani Army stepped in. In January 1948, Pandit Nehru referred the conflict to the UN. A ceasefire followed. A line of control was established. Jammu and Kashmir was divided into Pakistan Occupied Kashmir (POK) and Indian state of Jammu and Kashmir. UN observers were deployed to supervise ceasefire. The UN recommended plebiscite to resolve the dispute. The Government of India did not accept plebiscite saying Pakistan had violated the plebiscite conditions. The dispute simmered on.

Pakistan became an Islamic Republic in 1956. Just two years later the military took control of the nation. Field Marshal Ayub Khan became president. Ayub took advantage of the cold war and established close relations with the US and the West. Pakistan joined two formal military alliances, the Baghdad Pact (later known as CEO) which included Iran, Iraq, and Turkey to defend the Middle East and the Persian Gulf against the Soviet Union and SEATO which covered South-East Asia. As a result, America provided substantial military aid in the form of small arms, tanks, anti-tank weapons, artillery, and fighter aircraft. This emboldened General Ayub Khan, Pakistani President to try to take Indian Kashmir by force. He attacked Kutch in May 1965 to draw part of the Indian Army to the South. He then attacked Jammu and Kashmir and Khemkaran in 1965. India under Prime Minister Lal Bahadur Shastri responded with attacks in Lahore Sector and Hajipir. Neither side made any decisive gains. A peace treaty was signed at Tashkent and both sides withdrew to old borders. UN observers withdrew.

During the general elections held in 1970, Awami League led by Sheikh Mujibur Rahaman won 160 out of 162 seats in East Pakistan. Pakistani Peoples Party led by Zulfikar Ali Bhutto won the most seats in West Pakistan. Bhutto tried to persuade Mujib to form a coalition government. Mujib insisted of becoming Prime Minister. A military crackdown started on 26 March 1970 in East Pakistan. Mujibur Rahaman and many Awami League leaders were arrested. However, Mujib managed to send out a hand written declaration of Independence. This declaration was made public on March 27, 1970. Pakistani Army tried to put down the independence struggle by a campaign of terror. Millions fled to India. Bengali military and paramilitary officers and men formed the Mukti Bahini and resisted. India provided military and financial aid to the Mukti Bahini which set up bases in India. In December 1971, India launched a military campaign and liberated East Pakistan in a 15-day war. Bangladesh was born. India captured over 90,000 Pakistani soldiers. Pakistan vowed to take revenge at place and time of its choosing.

When India attacked East Pakistan, Pakistan attacked India in the West. These attacks were beaten back by Indian Army. Ceasefire took place after the surrender at Dhaka. Pakistan made another attempt to capture Kashmir in 1999. In this battle, known as the Kargil War, the Pakistani's were again defeated after making initial gains. Pakistan has been using terrorism in Jammu and Kashmir as a weapon to weaken India. It also provided assistance to terrorists in North East India through Bangladesh when General Ershad overthrew the India friendly Awami League Government and ruled Bangladesh till his death.

An insurgency movement started in Jammu and Kashmir in 1989. Pakistan took advantage of the situation and supported the insurgency by providing sanctuaries, financial and military aid, and training. Pakistan's ISI recruit's terrorist in Pakistan for fighting in India. Its ISI was involved in attacks by Pakistani terrorists within India. It continues to do so even today.

China Befriends Pakistan

Defence cooperation between Pakistan and China began in 1963 when Pakistan ceded a part of Pakistan Occupied Kashmir (POK) in the Karakorum mountains as a part of their border settlement pact of March 3, 1963. Since then, China has emerged as Pakistan's single most trusted and enduring military ally. Pakistan is a major market for Chinese weapons and products. China supplies Pakistan with cheap products and technologies. It also provides the required political, moral, and financial support to Pakistan when required. In return Pakistan gives China access to western technologies that arrive in Pakistan. It also gives China vital access to the Arabian Sea.

The United States stopped military aid to both India and Pakistan during the Indo – Pak War of 1965 and again when the two countries tested atomic weapons. This pushed Pakistan closer towards China in an attempt to diversify its sources of weapons and other equipment. Pakistan defied considerable American pressure to seek a strategic relationship with China. China provided diplomatic support to Pakistan in its war with India in 1965 and 1971.

The first formal step towards Sino-Pak defence cooperation was taken soon after 1965 war between India and Pakistan. China provided technical and financial assistance for setting up an ordnance factory at Dhaka, East Pakistan. Several factories for producing defence equipment were set up with the help of Chinese assistance and expertise. China aided Pakistan in setting up facilities for the overhauling of Chinese tanks, and license production of the Chinese Tanks and BMPs. Pakistan's missile development program was started in the 1986 when Pakistan started assembling the Chinese RBS-70 Mk 1 and Mk 2 air defence missiles systems. Pakistan successfully tested its Hatf II missile with a 300 km range in 1989. China has also provided significant assistance to Pakistan's ballistic missile program in the year 2000 which has put the country on the road to serial production of Short-Range Ballistic Missiles like Shaheen-1 and Haider-1.

China has supplied Pakistan with more than 1,600 main battle tanks, 400 combat aircraft and about 40 naval vessels. In 2017, Pakistan Army imported Chinese-built Low to Medium Altitude Air Defence System for its air defence system. The Pakistani air force has been supplied with F-6 fighters, Q-5 fighters, F-7 fighter bombers and IL28 bombers. The F-7 are multi role combat aircraft with a range of 850km and can reach most cities in north west India. JF17 fighters and J-10 fighters (based on American F 16 design) have also been supplied. The Pakistani navy has been supplied with 12 Shanghai Class patrol boats, 4 Hainan Class patrol boats, 4 Huchan class and 4 Hegu Class fast attack craft and 2 Romeo class destroyers, and four F-22 frigates. The Chinese are also helping Pakistan in developing one of its key naval bases at Gwadar, which is strategically located at the mouth of the Strait of Hormuz. The Chinese Navy has access to this port. It gives the Chinese warships and submarines a base to operate from in the Arabian Sea. China and Pakistan are involved in several projects to enhance military and weaponry systems, which include the joint development of the JF-17 Thunder fighter aircraft, K-8 Karakoram advanced jet trainer and AAWAC systems, Al-Khalid tanks based on the Chinese Type 90 and/or MBT-2000. The Chinese has designed tailor-made advanced weapons for Pakistan.

China helped Pakistan become a nuclear weapons power. China-Pakistan nuclear cooperation began in the early 1980s. In 1983, China had transferred a complete nuclear weapon design to Pakistan, along with enough weapon grade uranium for two nuclear weapons. It was because of Chinese assistance that Pakistan could carry out successful nuclear weapons tests within a day of India's nuclear tests on 26 May 1998. Pakistan's Chashma Nuclear Power Plant, which is built by Chinese firms, was commissioned in November 1999. China continues providing equipment and technology for the construction of a 40 MW reactor at Khushab. The reactor provides Pakistan with weapon grade plutonium for its weapons program.

Pakistan and China have agreed to build first ever train routes along the Karakorum Highway. China may be interested in the oil and gas reserves in Baluchistan province of Pakistan. The Karakorum Highway linking northern Pakistan to Western China through Pakistan Occupied Kashmir and the Khunjareb Pass was completed in 1978.

China and Pakistan have signed a multi-billion China Pakistan Economic Corridor (CPEC) agreement. The CPEC will connect Pakistan with China and the Central Asian countries with modern highways, railways and oil pipelines. It will connect Kashgar in Xinjian Province through Karakoram Pass to Gwadar Port Baluchistan Province of Pakistan. Gwadar Port will serve as the trade nerve centre for China. Most of its trade including oil with Middle East will be done through the port. The port is operated by the China Overseas Port Holding Company, a state-owned Chinese company.

Present Situation

Imran Khan became the Prime Minister of Pakistan when his party, Tehreek-e-Islam won the general election in 2018. In 2020, Pakistan's Prime Minister, Imran Khan drew up a new map of Pakistan showing POK and ex-princely state of Junagadh as Pakistani territory. He also insisted that the only solution to the Kashmir problem was as per UN Resolution 39 of January 1948. India protested.

Relations between the Pakistani Army and Imran Khan soured over the appointment of the ISI Chief. In 2022, the opposition parties brought a no confidence motion against him and ousted him with the help of the Pakistani Army. Countrywide protests followed with many army assets being torched by the protestors. On 19 April 2022, Mr. Shahbaz Sharif became the new PM. However, popular protests by Imran's party continued and was brutally put down by the Army. Imran Khan and his wife have been convicted in a corruption case and sentenced to 15 years in jail. Political turmoil continues unabated.

Pakistan's economy is registering a nosedive on major economic indicators. The country's trade deficit stands at 12 billion dollars, which is the highest ever in its 61year old history. Pakistan's Prime Minister, Imran Khan has approached China for help to tide over its financial problems in February 2022. China has promised to help cash strapped Pakistan avert a financial disaster. Pakistan has no means to earn the foreign exchange required to pay back China. It is somehow surviving with an IMF loan. The only way it can payback China is by giving Gilgit and Baltistan in Pakistani Occupied Kashmir on 99 years lease in the same way as Sri Lanka has given away Hambantota.

Baloch separatist insurgency started in 1948 and has ebbed and flowed ever since. Baluchistan Liberation Army has become active since 2000. Since then, there have been regular attacks on military and para-military forces, civil administration, non-Baloch's, and Chinese national working on projects. The situation has worsened with Baluch Liberation Army getting military and financial support from Afghanistan. They have launched multiple attacks including hijacking a train and taking hostages. Pakistan has accused India of aiding the Baluchs.

Terrorism in Pakistan's Khyber Pakhtunkhwa Province started in 2004. Tehreek-i-Taliban, Pakistan (TTP) is the main insurgent group. They have posed a serious challenge to the Pakistani Army. They have bases in Afghanistan and carry out raids into Pakistan at will.

Pakistan has started escalating terrorism in Kashmir. The Pahalgam massacre has added a new dimension to the relationship between the two countries. India has promised to end cross border terrorism. It will be interesting to see how that is achieved and when.

Summary

Pakistan-India relations are at its nadir. Trade between the two nations has stopped. Train services, bus services, cultural exchanges have also stopped. Pakistan continues to provide military and financial aid to terrorists operating in Jammu and Kashmir. It provides shelter to Khalistani separatists. With the fall of Sheikh Hasina Government in Bangladesh, Pakistan has rushed to establish close relations with the Yunus Government and between the two armies.

China has long been one of Pakistan's closest regional partners, with Beijing looking to Islamabad as a counterbalance to India. China is the only country in the world that has helped Pakistan both economically and militarily. Chinese presence at Gwadar would help Chinese to keep track of US naval ships in the Gulf. Pakistan is also the geopolitical hub for bringing China, the Gulf including Iran and Africa into a thriving economic interaction.

Analysis

Pakistan has a pathological hatred for India. It will continue to aid terrorists and separatists in Kashmir. It will also use its new found leverage with Bangladesh to try to revive insurgencies in north east India. The Manipur conflict offers it an opportunity to do so. Hindutva imposition like banning beef and cow slaughter, detecting, and deporting illegal immigrants from Bangla Desh, and likely introduction of Uniform Civil Code also provides an opportunity to exploit minority apprehensions of both Muslims, Christians, and tribal population of the North-East.

The Pakistani Army is fighting insurgencies in Baluchistan and Khyber Pakhtunkhwa Provinces. It is also struggling to contain the civil unrest created periodically by the supporters of Imran Khan. **Pakistan does not have the military or economic capability to fight India in a conventional war.**

It is possible that China will take advantage of this hatred and try get Pakistan to help it militarily to cut India to size at an appropriate time. China has maintained that Kashmir is disputed territory. It has opposed India's reorganization of the State of Jammu and Kashmir. India is actively trying to take back POK. China has invested billions of dollars to build a communication network through POK to connect Gwadar Port to Xinjiang. **I do not see any prospect of China allowing POK to join India. Any attempt by India to take POK by military action will certainly result in war with China.**

Some kind of military action against Pakistan to avenge the Pahalgam massacre seems imminent. How Pakistan and its allies, China, Turkey, and Bangladesh respond will decide whether the war will be short or

long. Pakistan has no option but to side with China if it decides to attack India.

CHAPTER THREE

Threat From China

Early Days

Relations between the two countries further soured in 1959 when Tibetan spiritual leader Dalai Lama fled communist persecution and was given asylum in India with 15,000 of his followers. Soon after, the border dispute worsened between the two countries. China claimed Aksai Chin in the western sector and India claimed territories south of the McMahon line in the eastern sector.

Border disputes resulted in a short border war between the People's Republic of China (PRC) and India. The war started on 20th October 1962. Within a few weeks, the Chinese Army pushed the ill-prepared, and inadequately led Indian forces to within forty-eight kms of the Assam plains. They consolidated their hold on Aksai Chin and occupied strategic points in Ladakh. China declared a unilateral cease fire on 21 November 1962 and withdrew twenty kms behind the actual line of control.

China diplomatically backed Pakistan in its 1965 war with India. Between 1967 and 197. An all-weather road was built in Pakistan Occupied Kashmir (POK) linking China's Xinjiang Province with Pakistan. India could do no more than protest. China supplied ideological, financial, weapons and training to dissident groups, especially to Naga insurgents in north eastern India. China also accused India of assisting the Khampa rebels in Tibet. Diplomatic contact between the two governments was minimal although not formally severed.

Border clashes continued to occur. In late 1967, there were two skirmishes between Indian and Chinese forces in Sikkim. The first one was dubbed the "Nathu La incident", and the other the "Chola incident". In the winter of 1986, the Chinese deployed their troops to the Sumdorong Chu before the Indian team could arrive in the summer and built a helipad at Wandung. Surprised by the Chinese occupation, Indian Army airlifted a brigade to the region. Chinese troops could not move any further into the valley and were forced to move sideways along the Thag La ridge, away from the valley.

India granted of statehood to Arunachal Pradesh in February 1987. This angered China. Both sides deployed new troops to the area, raising tensions and fears of a new border war. China sent out warnings that it would "teach India a lesson" if it did not cease "nibbling" at Chinese territory. Both sides had backed away from conflict by the summer of 1987and denied that military clashes had taken place.

Improvement in Relations

Improvement in relations between the two countries was facilitated by Rajeev Gandhi's visit to China in December 1988. It was the first visit by an Indian prime minister to China since Nehru's 1954 visit.The two sides issued a joint communique that stressed the need to restore friendly relations on the basis of the principles of "Panch Sheel". Rajeev Gandhi signed bilateral agreements on cooperation in science and technology, on civil aviation to establish direct air links and on cultural exchanges.

The mid-1990s showed a slow but steady improvement in relations with China. Top level dialog continued with the December 1991 visit of Chinese premier Li Peng to India and the May 1992 visit to China of Indian President R Venkataraman. Progress was also made in reducing tensions on the border via confidence-building measures, including mutual troop reductions, regular meetings of local military commanders and advance notification of military exercises. Border trade resumed in July 1992 after a gap of more than thirty years. Consulates reopened in Mumbai and Shanghai in 1992. The two sides agreed to open an additional border trading post in 1993.

Prime Minister Narsimha Rao and Premier Li Peng signed the border agreement and three other agreements on cross-border trade, on increased cooperation on environment and in radio and television broadcasting during the formers visit to Beijing in September 1993. A senior level Chinese military delegation made a six-day goodwill visit to India in December 1993. India ignored reports that China was exporting greater amounts of military material to Burma's army, navy and air force and sending an increasing number of technicians to Burma. Indian authorities also played down the presence of Chinese radar technicians in Burma's Coco Islands,which border the Andaman and Nicobar Islands. The 1993 Chinese military delegation's visit to India was reciprocated by Indian army chief of staff in 1994. The border issue was raised in September 1994 when

Chinese defence minister visited New Delhi for extensive talks with high-level Indian trade and defence officials. Further talks were held in New Delhi in March 1995 by the India-China Expert Group. The two sides were reported to be "seriously engaged" in defining the McMahon Line and the LAC. Mr. George Fernandes, then defence minister visited China in 1996. Zhang Zemin, the chairman of the Central Military Commission in 1996, greeted Mr. Fernandes in an unprecedented gesture. During the Kargil war, the Chinese stance was a tacit acceptance of the LOC in Jammu and Kashmir as the international border.

Relations Sour Again

India China relations nosedived again in May 1998 after India conducted nuclear tests. Mr. George Fernandes was widely quoted as having said that China is India's enemy number one. But he consistently denied ever having made such a statement. India also accused China of supporting Pakistan's nuclear and missile programs. Relations between India and China stayed strained until the end of the decade.

Relations Improve Again

Indian President K R Narayana visited China in 2000. This marked a gradual diplomatic re-engagement of India and China. In 2002, Chinese Premier Zhu Rongji reciprocated the President's visit by visiting India with a focus on economic issues. 2003 ushered in a marked improvement in Sino-Indian relations following Indian Prime Minister Atal Bihari Vajpayee's visit to China in June 2003. China officially recognized Indian sovereignty over Sikkim as the two nations moved toward resolving their border disputes.

2004 also witnessed a gradual improvement in relations. The Nathu La and Jelep La passes in Sikkim were opened for border trade. 2004 was a milestone in Sino-Indian bilateral trade which surpassed the $10 billion mark for the first time. In April 2005, Chinese Premier Wen Jiabao visited Bangalore to push for increased Sino-Indian cooperation in high-tech industries. The high-level visit produced several agreements to deepen political, cultural and economic ties between the two nations. But China has not supported India on the issue of India gaining a permanent seat on the UN Security Council. China was granted an observer status in the SAARC Summit of 2005. While other countries in the region are ready to consider China for permanent membership in the SAARC, India is reluctant.

On Jan. 14, 2008, during his first official visit to Beijing, India Prime Minister Manmohan Singh sat down with Chinese Premier Wen Jiabao in the Great Hall of the People to emphasize what the two Asian giants have in common. The leaders signed a seven-page document that covers issues such as their fast-growing economic ties, defence cooperation, anti-terrorism efforts, climate change and energy policies. Noting that India and China "are the two largest developing nations on earth representing more than one-third of humanity," the document goes on to note that the countries with a history of mutual suspicion are now "convinced that it is time to look to the future in building a relationship," and that "China India friendship and common development will have a positive influence on the future of the world."

An inter-governmental organization of five countries, Brazil, Russia, India, China, and South Africa called BRICKS was formed in 2009 to be a counter to economic domination by G-7 countries. It has been expanded to include Egypt, Ethiopia, Indonesia, Iran, and United Arab Emirates.

Renewal of Tensions

BJP came to power in 2014 and Mr. Narendra Modi became Prime Minister. Mr. Modi tried to improve relations with China. He invited the Chinese President Xi Jinping to his home state, Gujarat. The Chinese President reciprocated the gesture by inviting Mr. Modi. However, the bonhomie remained visual. China has stubbornly refused to allow India entry into the Nuclear Suppliers Group. It has vetoed UN proposal to declare Mumbai terror attack mastermind Hafeez Saeed a global terrorist. Under Xi, China has displayed strong expansionist tendencies in South China Sea and against India. It has given Tibetan names to six towns in Arunachal Pradesh in its maps.

The 2017 standoff between the two armies at Doklam Plateau south of Chumbi Valley of Tibet show no sign of ending. Doklam plateau is a disputed territory between China and Bhutan. It is recognized by India as belonging to Bhutan. As per China's new assertive and aggressive policy it started building a road from Yadong to the region and destroyed two India bunkers at Doka La. The confrontation ended with Indian troops pulling back to their original position at Doka La in August 2017. China has quietly improved the road communication to Doklam and built accommodation for troops and stores. It is reported to have about 1600 troops in the region. **(Source: waronrocks.com; "Doklam: one year later. China's long game in the Himalayas" by Joel Wuthnow, Satu Limaye and Nilanthi Samaranyeke, June 17, 2018).** Indian and Bhutanese Governments are keeping quiet.

Beginning on 5 May 2020, Chinese and Indian troops were engaged in a face-off at locations along LAC in Ladakh. In late May, Chinese forces objected to Indian road construction in the Galwan River valley. Chinese and Indian troops clashed on 15/16 June 2020. The incident resulted in the deaths of 20 Indian soldiers. Casualties on the Chinese side was not declared. On 7 September, shots were fired along the LAC for the first time in 45 years. Both sides blamed each other for the incident. Partial disengagement from Galwan, Hot Springs, and Gogra occurred in June–July 2020. Complete disengagement from Pangong Lake north and south bank took place in February 2021. China has changed the status quo on the North Bank of Pangong Tso. It tried to capture heights on the south bank of Pangong Tso and were thwarted by timely occupation of the features like Gurung Hill and Rezangla. It has been building new military infrastructures like airfields, radar installations, missile bases, ammunition and logistic depots and accommodation for troops all along the LAC from Ladakh to Arunachal. It is now building a bridge across Pangong Tso. Our trade deficit continues to fund China's growing defence budget. There has been some softening of stand by the Chinese recently. Patrolling by both sides have been agreed to in the areas of Daulat Beg Oldie and Depsang. Let us see how long the détente lasts.

The relations between the two countries have shown some improvement in 2024 with some agreements regarding border patrolling along LAC in Ladakh. Trade relations have remained good, possibly because China enjoys over $ 50 billion trade surplus. Whether this consideration and both being members of BRICKS will ensure peace between the two countries remains to be seen.

China's Counter India Strategy

Beijing's "counter-India" strategy was drawn up in the 1950s. India was identified as an eventual competitor for being the pre-eminent power in Asia. The Chinese strategy is to encircle India by a ring of countries friendly to China. China aligned with Pakistan as early as 1963 and has been a major supplier of military equipment, technology, and economic aid since then.

It next aligned with Bangladesh in 1976 and was the primary supplier of military equipment during the BNP Regime and provides financial aid to Bangladesh. However, with change in political power in Bangladesh in 2008, Chinese influence in Bangladesh had waned. Now with Sheikh Hasina and her Awami Leage government overthrown, China and Pakistan are back in power and ready with their anti-Indian activities.

China next aligned with the Military Junta ruling Myanmar in 1988. Chinese military and economic aid have enabled the Military Junta in Myanmar to defy the US and the West and continue with its autocratic regime. But its overthrow of the democratically elected government of Ang Sang Soichi has led to a civil war that the Army is not winning.

China aligned with Sri Lanka in its battle with the LTTE in 2004. It has supplied military equipment and aid to Sri Lanka and encouraged Pakistan to do the same. It is providing economic aid and assisting Sri Lanka in developing its infrastructure and oil and gas resources. China has developed many infrastructure projects in Sri Lanka like the Hambantota Port and Airport and Colombo.

It has increased its influence in Nepal with the Communists coming to power. Bhutan is the only SAARC nation other than India which is not in the Chinese camp. China is known to have denied India membership of the APEC. It also tried to keep India outside the ASEAN and the ASEAN Regional Forum (ARF). China opposes India getting a seat in the UN Security Council.

Indo – US Defence Cooperation

Beijing makes no secret of its perception that it considers India to be a part of US plans to encircle China. China believes that the Indo-US defence cooperation was to counter China's regional aspirations and the US intended to form a strategic partnership with India to increase its influence in South Asia to counter China. It also considers that the US-India nuclear co-operation was part of India's ambition to become a super power and its conventional defence build-up was aimed to dominate South Asia. India's membership of QUAD and military and economic relations with Vietnam, Taiwan and Philippines has made China more hostile.

Moderating Influences on China

Both India and China are founding members of the BRICKS alliance established in 2001 which also includes Russia, Brazil, and South Africa. It is an alliance for economic cooperation. It has also its own bank like the Asian Development Bank. The alliance has recently expanded to include ten other countries. President Trump is worried that the alliance will try to create a new currency or trade in currencies other than the US dollar and thus reduce its dominance. This alliance and Russia have a moderating influence on Indo-China relations. The other factor which goes against China launching all-out war on India is its huge trade surplus of over $ 50 billion. China's economy will suffer if its trade with India stops due to war.

However, war does not always stop trade. EU is at war with Russia for all practical purposes over Ukraine but buys Russian oil and gas. EU needs the oil and Russia needs the money.

Infrastructure Development in Tibet

China has been improving the connectivity between main land China and Tibet ever since it annexed Tibet in 1950. It has built five networks of roads leading to its borders with India and Nepal. **The Western Highway or the Xinjiang -Tibet Highway.** This network starts at Amdo and passes through Silling - Aksai Chin and connects Tibet with Xinjiang Province's road-network at Mazar. **Qinghai-Tibet Highway.** This network is Tibet's longest asphalt paved road. It stretches from Xining, the capital city of Qinghai Province to Lhasa. It has gradual gradients and is of high quality. It is the safest road to Tibet. **Sichuan-Tibet Highway.** This highway runs between Chengdu, the capital city of Sichuan Province and Lhasa. Sichuan-Tibet Highway is probably the most dangerous highway in the world. It has two branches. The North Route is about 2,400 km long and the South Route of about 2,100 km. It runs across a variety of rivers and mountains with the highest point over 5,000 m above sea level. Landslides are frequent. The road is very susceptible to attack by the Indian Air Force or disruption by Tibetan resistance. **The Yunnan-Tibet Highway.** This highway connects Yunnan Province to Tibet. It skirts Arunachal Pradesh from the East and will be used if China decides to attack Lohit or Subansari districts of Arunachal Pradesh or for moving troops from Yunnan Province to Tibet. **The Sino-Nepal Highway** is the only international highway in Tibet. It connects Lhasa to Kathmandu. **Highway S 207.** This highway runs east from Shigatze up to Dingxiang and then turns south towards Yadong valley and Dokalam. This is the main supply route for troops deployed opposite Sikkim and Western Bhutan. **Highway G 318/G 4218.** This starts at Yaan in Sichuan Province of China and runs west along the border with Arunachal Pradesh and on to Lasha. **Highway G 219.** This highway starts at Lasha and runs west via Shigatze all along the border with India. It turns north on crossing the Indus River and enters Aksai Chin and goes to Xinjian. This is the main supply route for Chinese troops deployed opposite Uttarakhand, Himachal Pradesh and Ladakh.

The Qinghai-Tibet railway is the longest and highest plateau-based railroad in the world. It has a total length of 1,956 km and connects Xining in Qinghai Province and Lhasa in the Tibet Autonomous Region. It was completed in 2006. China claims that the annual transport capacity of the railway was 5 million tons per year or about 14,000 tons per day.

The Golmud - Lhasa pipeline has a capacity of half a million tons of fuel annually. With the completion of the Qinghai-Tibet railway line, China will be able to overcome a major obstacle to increasing its military deployment near the India-Tibet border region. Some consider that the rail link gives China the capability to induct up to 12 divisions a month into Tibet.

Tibet has 25 airfields and air strips. All the airfields in Tibet have been lengthened and upgraded. Many air bases have been built. Currently only four are in active use but others can be activated in a short period of time. **China's PLAAF has fourteen military airfields and bases in Tibet. These are Taxcorgan, Ngari-Gunsa, Burang, Tingri, Shigatse, Lasha-Gongar, Damxung, Lhuntse, Hoping, Pangta, Shiquanhe, and Kong Ka. Of these Ngari-Gunsa, Shigatse and Lhuntse are withing 60 km of Tibet's border with China.**

Summary

Historical relations between India and China have been largely restricted to trade and cultural exchanges. But post 1950, their relations have been plagued by border disputes, Dalai Lama, Tibet, and regional rivalry. There are some issues between the two countries which are difficult to resolve.

The first and most pressing problem is the territorial dispute. Both neighbours claim that the other occupies territory that is rightfully theirs.

The second insolvable problem is the presence of Dalai Lama and Tibetan refugees in India. China sees these people as a potential threat to its hold over Tibet. It is impossible for India to deport Dalai Lama and the Tibetan refugees to Tibet.

There are other problems too. India cannot ignore of China's military alliances with Pakistan, Bangladesh, Sri Lanka, Myanmar, and Nepal. It also cannot ignore China's development of military infrastructure and troop deployments along the LAC which pose serious military threats.

China has its own worries. It was none too pleased with the QUAD, an alliance of USA, Japan, Australia, and India created by President Donald Trump to preserve South China Sea as international waters. Beijing believes the close co-operation between these four countries was directed against China. India's growing closeness to the U.S., including the India-U.S. nuclear cooperation, has made China nervous.

Relations between China and India are at its worst in recent years. The bonhomie between Mr. Modi and Mr. Xi Jinping of 2014 has not endured. The armies of the two countries are in eyeball-to-eyeball contact in Ladakh and in high state of alert in other areas. War can break out at any moment.

China continues to improve its military logistics and infrastructure along the LAC. It is continually improving roads to the LAC and building dual purpose villages along the LAC which hold military hardware, ammunition and fuel and can also house Chinese troops. Since July 2017, the government of China's Tibet Autonomous Region has been constructing hundreds of border villages and accompanying infrastructure as part of a major push to develop China's remote border regions. Between 2018 and 2022, the region is said to have built 624 such villages. Many of these are clustered along the Lac in Arunachal. (**Source: www.chinapower.csic.org/ analysis/china-upgrading-dual-use-xiakong-villages-india-border).**

China under Xi Jinping has passed a new law making it territorial claims non-negotiable. There is no possibility of resolving the boundary issue unless both countries are ready to accept the LAC as the international border. As of today, this is highly unlikely. In fact, the indications are quite to the contrary.

Analysis

India cannot prevent China from being friendly with its neighbours and providing them with military equipment, military, and economic aid. No amount of sugar coating or rhetoric can hide the insurmountable nature of the problems to developing friendly relations between the two countries. The only option before India is to make itself militarily and economically strong enough to make China averse to a military adventure against it.

China is ready to attack India. Is Indian Armed Forces ready to defend India?

CHAPTER FOUR

Threat From Bangladesh

China was against secession of East Pakistan and the struggle for independence launched by the people of Bangladesh. China supported Pakistan against the Mukti Bahini during the Bangladesh Liberation War of 1971 but did not intervene militarily. In 1972, China exercised its veto power as a permanent member of the UN Security Council to block Bangladesh's entry into the UN. Bangladesh under Sheikh Mujibur Rehman had aligned itself with India. After the fall of Sheikh Hasina's Government in August 2024, the Yunus Government is aligned with Pakistan and China. China is the first foreign country he visited in March 2025.

1975 - 2008

Following the assassination of Mujibur and overthrow of the Awami League government in 1975 Pakistan warmed towards Bangladesh and diplomatic relations were established between the two countries in 1975-76. Pakistan's allies such as Saudi Arabia and China followed suit. An agreement between China and Bangladesh to establish diplomatic and economic relations was signed in late 1975 and duly ratified in 1976. The then president of Bangladesh, Ziaur Rahaman, made an official visit to China in 1977. By the mid-1980s, China had forged close commercial and cultural ties with Bangladesh and supplied it with military aid and equipment. In 2002, the Chinese Premier Wen Jiabao made an official visit to Bangladesh and both countries declared 2005 as the "Bangladesh-China Friendship Year."

China made serious attempts to wean over Bangladesh from India's influence. Bangladesh became a part of the Chinese game plan to encircle India. Bangladesh thus became a major recipient of Chinese arms. China has assured Bangladesh of enhanced military and economic assistance. Bangladesh on its part endorsed the one China policy of Beijing.

In 2006, Dhaka emerged as one of the prime buyers of weapons made in China. China sold 65 large calibre artillery systems, 16 combat aircraft and 114 missiles and related equipment to Bangladesh in 2005 besides small arms and 82 mm mortars. In 2008 Bangladesh set up a missile launch pad near the Chittagong Port with assistance from China. Bangladesh performed its maiden missile test on May 12, 2008 with active participation of Chinese experts. It successfully test-fired a ship based anti-ship cruise missile C-802 A with a strike range of 120 km from a frigate near Kutubdia Island in the Bay of Bengal. The frigate was a 1500-ton Chinese built Jianghu class warship commissioned into the Bangladesh Navy and the C-802A missile, according to experts, is a modified version of Chinese Ying Ji missile.

Bangladesh-China Defence Co-operation

A Defence Co-operation Agreement was signed between Bangladesh and China during the visit of Bangladesh Prime Minister, Begum Khaleda Zia to China in 2002. The new agreement was to help institutionalize the existing accords in defence sector and to consolidate the existing piecemeal agreements to enhance cooperation in training, maintenance and some areas in production that had existed since the early eighties. The purpose of Defence Cooperation Agreement was to meet present day up gradation and modernization needs of Bangladesh's defence forces. It was claimed that this defence umbrella agreement was not directed against any country and would not affect Bangladesh's relations with India.

The agreement also helps Pakistan's strategic designs against India because Bangladesh's enhanced military profile with Chinese aid would divert some of India's strategic military assets from the West to the East and lower the pressure on Pakistan. Rising Islamic fundamentalism in Bangladesh makes it easier to use Bangladesh territory for intensifying Pakistan's proxy war on India's Eastern peripheries.

China's strategic interests are also served by the Bangladesh-China Defence Cooperation Agreement. As a result of the Agreement, China gets a strategic toe hold on India's Eastern flank in Bangladesh. China's strategic encirclement of India is enhanced through the treaty. China could start developing the Chittagong Naval Base on the lines of Gwadar in Pakistan and in return get naval bases facility in Bangladesh.

2008 to 2024

Awami League returned to power in the 2008 general election. Sheikh Hasina became the Prime Minister. The 2014 General election was boycotted by BNP and other opposition parties. Awami League won a landslide victory. The 2018 General election was marred by allegations of vote rigging. Awami League again won a landslide victory. Anti-India trend has somewhat reduced with the pro India Awami League coming to power. Seikh Hasina tried to reduce dependency on Chinese weapon systems by purchasing arms in Europe.

Aug 2024 to Date

Sheikh Hasina won her fourth consecutive term when her party, the Awami League, won 224 of the 300 parliamentary seats amidst a low voter turnout in an election boycotted by the main opposition.

In June 2024, Sheikh Hasina visited India. This was followed by a visit to China in July 2024. Protests broke out during the same month over reforms to a quota system in Government jobs. Following attempts by the government to put down the protests by strong arm tactics, the protests turned violent resulting in over 2000 plus deaths and more than 20,000 injuries. On 3 August, the protest organizers issued a single demand calling for the resignation of Sheikh Hasina and her cabinet. Under pressure from the Army, Hasina resigned on 5 August 2024. Her resignation was announced by the Chief of the Army Staff. Later that day, Hasina fled to India and is living there since then. Sheikh Hasina was living in a secret location in India under tight security as of August 2024. (**Source: en.wikipedia.org/wiki/government_of_bangladesh**). Bangladesh is now run by an interim government headed by Professor Yunus and ministers appointed by him which has the backing of the Bangladesh Amy. There is a systematic purge of members of the Awami League and Sheikh Mujibur's relatives. There are also reports of large scale vandalizations of Hindu religious places, institutions, and homes.

Implications for India

The fall of Sheikh Hasina government is a significant setback for India's security. Under Hasina's rule, a secular Bangladesh, eradicated training camps used by Indian separatist rebels and helped end the decades-long insurgency in India's turbulent northeastern region. Bangladesh actively countered Pakistan's Inter-Services Intelligence (ISI) network. It adopted a tough counter-terrorism policy against the Harkat-ul-Jihad al-Islami Bangladesh terror group in 2017. All that is changed. ISI Chief has visited Bangladesh. (**source: iiss.org/online-analysis/2024/8/Bangladesh-in-turmoil**). Senior Bangladesh generals have visited Pakistan. This changes the threat perception from Bangladesh.

Militarization of Bangladesh

General Ershad took over as president of Bangladesh in 1982 and remained in power till 1991. He modernized and strengthened the Bangladesh Army with military aid from Pakistan and China. The strength of the Army rose to seven divisions. Bangladesh Army sent a 2,193-member team to monitor peace in Saudi Arabia and Kuwait during the First Gulf War 1991. The Bangladesh Army also participated in peace keeping activities in many countries. As of October 2008, Bangladesh remained the second largest contributor with 9,800 troops in the UN Peacekeeping forces. The Bangladeshi military engaged in counter-insurgency operations in the Chittagong Hill Tracts against the Shanti Bahini, a separatist group. In 2001, Bangladeshi military units clashed with the Indian Border Security Force (BSF) along its northern border.

After General Ershad, several projects to expand and modernize the Bangladeshi armed forces were launched by his wife and successor, Begum Khalida Zia. After coming to power in 2008, Sheikh Hasina launched a modernization program for Bangladesh Armed Force called "Forces Goal 2030." Under this program, the strength of the Bangladesh Army was raised by three new divisions, bringing the number of divisions to 10.

Standoffs between Bangladesh Army and Myanmar Army occasionally occurred at the border in 1991 and 2008. Most of the standoffs took place, when Myanmar attempted to force Rohingya's into Bangladesh. In 2008, the two countries deployed warships after Myanmar attempted to explore a disputed Bay of Bengal seabed for oil and gas. The dispute was resolved at an international tribunal in 2012. In 2015, Bangladesh Army and Arakan Army also clashed at the border.

As Sun Tzu said, one should not rely on intentions of a nation but on its military capability. Intentions can change with change of government. But it takes a lot of time and money to build a viable deterrence. Chinese may be back in Bangladesh in any conflict with India.

Summary

Bangladesh was created in December 1971 when India defeated the Pakistan Army in erstwhile East Pakistan and handed over power to Sheikh Mujibur Rehman, its first Prime Minister. **In spite this, Bangladesh has been unfriendly to India whenever Awami League is not in power.** As Bangladesh had been a part of Pakistan and has a predominantly Muslim population, it draws its political and strategic ideologies from Pakistan and Saudi Arabia. Like Pakistan, Bangladesh's politics get defined in the context of anti-India stances.

Like Pakistan, Bangladesh had come under growing influence of Islamic fundamentalists. During the past government of Begum Khaleda Zia, the Jamaat group was part of the ruling coalition. **Bangladesh shares a long and porous 3901 kms border with India.** This has enabled more than 2 million Bangladeshi nationals to move into India as illegal immigrants. India is rounding up these immigrants and putting them in detention camps. Will Bangladesh accept these people when deported? Any attempt to deport Bangladeshis will escalate tensions between the two countries.

Bangladesh offers Pakistan a fertile ground for basing its proxy war apparatus to strategically weaken India on its East and North Eastern peripheries. This arises from common religious links and shared heritage of its intelligence and military establishments with those of Pakistan.

Bangladesh has a strong army of ten divisions. Since the fall of Sheikh Hasina Government, the relations between India and Bangladesh have been strained. **There are three main problems between the two countries; deportation of illegal Bangladeshi immigrants from India, treatment of Hindu minorities in Bangladesh, stoppage of border trade and trade imbalance.** The presence of Sheikh Hasina in India adds to the tensions.

Analysis

The Pakistan-China strategic nexus in South Asia can come into play in Bangladesh. The Bangladesh-China Defence Cooperation is a result of this geopolitical environment. **The fall of Awami League government favourably disposed towards India, has encouraged Pakistan and China to take advantage of the situation and restart anti-India activities using Bangladesh territory.** The growing military cooperation between China and Bangladesh including the Bangladesh-China Defence Cooperation Agreement has serious strategic and tactical implications for India.

Bangladesh's Chief Advisor Prof. Mohammad Yunus while winding up his four-day trip to China said on 29 March 2025, "We are the only guardian of the ocean for all this region. So, this opens up a huge possibility. So, this could be an extension of the Chinese economy. Build things, produce things, market things, bring things to China, bring it out to the whole rest of the world," he said. **For India, access to and from the Northeast states — through the 'Chicken's Neck' corridor in north Bengal — has been a challenge,** economically and strategically. Over the last decade-and-a-half, this formed an important element of Delhi's engagement with Dhaka as it worked with the previous government led by former Prime Minister Sheikh Hasina on ways to transit through Bangladesh. (**Source:**

indianexpress .com/article/Yunus-pitch-to-china ......). India'srelations with Bangladesh is at present at its nadir.

India's threat perception and defence preparedness must take into account the regime change in Bangladesh and the growing military strength of Bangladesh army and air force. It must also recognize that Indo-Bangladesh relations are not cordial. Providing asylum to Sheikh Hasina presents a threat to the present regime. There is also resentment in Bangladesh over repatriation of illegal Bangladeshi Immigrants. Bangladesh faces serious economic challenges. They know that only China can and will bail them out. It is most likely that Bangladesh under the present regime will assist China and Pakistan in any military adventure against India.

CHAPTER FIVE

Lessons from Ukraine and Middle East Wars

Ukraine War

The wars in Ukraine and Gaza have many lessons for military strategists. In this book we will discuss only a few, use of air power and drones, failure of Russian battlefield surveillance, and inability of air defence systems to stop missiles and drones.

Use of Air Power

Russian air power, its fighter aircraft and attack helicopters played a prominent role in the initial stages of the Ukraine War. They also made good propaganda on televisions around the world. But as the war continued and air defence systems arrived from NATO, casualties mounted and use of fighter aircraft and attack helicopters reduced significantly. Air force has three roles; air combat for control of the air over the battle field, interdiction or isolation of the battle field from rear areas and logistic support by destroying roads, railways, bridges etc. and close air support to ground troops. In this role, the air force uses both fighter and attack helicopters to destroy enemy artillery, armoured vehicles and softening enemy defences. In Ukraine, the Ukraine air force is almost non-existent. Hence, Russian air force is not required for the purpose. Russia has stopped using aircraft for interdiction as drones and missiles are more cost effective. A new weapon being used is the "Glide bombs" which are launched from aircraft flying within Russian or Russian held areas. Main role of Russian air force is close air support to ground troops. Third generation fighter and bomber aircraft are adequate for this role. Drones are also being used in this role.

I consider India's need for fifth or sixth generation aircraft for air combat role is limited. These fighters costing $ 40 to 100 million are not cost effective. They are good for showing off and quite useless in limited wars with China and Pakistan. The air chief's comments on the capabilities of Hindustan Aeronautics Limited shows his bias and is quite disappointing. **It is this attitude in our senior military leaders that will keep India dependent on foreign countries for our defence equipment for ever.** The Ukraine War clearly shows is what India needs are large numbers of new third generation fighters preferably indigenously made and lots of drones and air defence capability.

Drones

Drones have played a significant role in the Ukraine war. Initially, Kamikaze drones which hit the target and explode supplied by Iran caused largescale casualties and destruction. Ukraine has developed its own drones and are able to reach over 800 km inside Russian territory. Neither Ukraine nor Russia have been able to shoot down more than 75% to 80% of the drones. The 20% to 25% drones that get through cause heavy damage to energy infrastructure, ammunition depots, ships, bridges. Ukraine aims to produce one million drones a year. They fire more than 100 drones at Russia every day. Effective use of drone requires an effective target acquisition system.

India's capabilities of producing and using drones and its battlefield target acquisition system is not in public domain. One can only hope that our armed forces have acquired adequate capability in this vital weapon system of modern warfare.

Failure of Russian Battlefield Surveillance

Ukraine launched a surprise offensive in the Kursk Region of Russia with a large force of 40,000 to 50,000 soldiers in August 2023 and captured over 1000 sq. km. of Russian territory. Ukrainian forces penetrated to a depth of 24 km into Russian territory. Russia's failure to detect the assembly of a large force on its border has cost it dear. It had to divert a large force from the Donbass region to first halt and then recapture lost territory. In the process, it suffered large casualties and loss of equipment like tanks, APCs, and artillery guns. Ukraine on the other hand is able to detect targets even at sea as the sinking of the Russian Baltic Sea Fleets flagship, the Markova demonstrated. This is due to intelligence and target information sharing by the US.

A similar failure by India to detect assembly of large Chinese forces around Yadong and Doklam and Bangladesh's forces opposite Siliguri-Jalpaiguri could lead to loss of the Siliguri Corridor and subsequently the entire North East. India needs to deploy satellite-based surveillance of

Yadong-Doklam and Northern Bangladesh.

Limitations of Air Defence Systems

As mentioned earlier, the air defence systems available to both Ukraine and Russia have been able to detect and destroy only 75% to 80% of enemy drones. Those that get through cause serious damage to energy infrastructures and logistic installations.

India's air defence capabilities have not been tested. The Russian S-400, the best that we have, has not been 100% effective against Ukrainian missiles and drones. In any case, it is difficult for a large country like ours to deploy adequate number of latest air-defence systems. India must take immediate steps to harden the logistic bases by taking them underground and camouflaging them to make their identification difficult.

Gaza War in Middle East

The Israel-Hamas-Hezbollah War has also thrown up many lessons. We will discuss only three, limitations of air defence systems, passive air defence and electronic warfare.

Limitations of Air Defence Systems

Israel has, arguably, the most formidable air defence system. The system consists of the "Iron Dome" range 70 km, "Thaad" supplied by the US with a range of up to 200 km, "David's Sling" with a range of up to 300 km and "Arrow" with a range of up to 2400 km. (**Source: CSIS Missile Threat, bbc.com/news/middle-east-20385306**). Despite this, missiles and drones fired by Hamas, Hezbollah, Houthis, and Iran occasionally get through and have even landed in Tel Aviv and Haifa. It will thus be seen that even the most elaborate air defence system cannot ensure 100% success in intercepting enemy missiles and drones. These systems are costly and ineffective against hypersonic missiles.

Air defence poses a serious challenge to India because of its large size and number of vulnerable areas which are within range of short and medium range missiles and drones in service with China, Pakistan, and Bangladesh. It is not cost effective for India to go in for expensive imported air defence systems like S 500 except for air defence of Delhi and its air bases. India must go in for cheaper passive air defences like tunnels, underground facilities, and camouflage.

Use of Helicopters in Anti Drone Role

Israel has repeatedly used helicopters to shoot down long-range drones fired from Iran or Yemen. This use of helicopters in air defence role merits serious consideration.

Passive Air Defence

Israel has pounded Gaza, Lebanon and Yemen with its air power, missiles, and drones for more than 500 days. It also has perhaps the most effective target acquisition systems in the world. Yet it has not been able to finish the fighting capabilities of Hamas, Hezbollah, Houthis, and Iran. This is due to the excellent passive air defence systems consisting of tunnels, and underground hangers which they have developed. They also have excellent damage management systems for fighting fires, rescuing people trapped under rubble and evacuation of the injured. Israel has an excellent system of early warning of incoming missiles and drones which gives time to citizen to get into shelters. Israel has also built underground hospitals to provide safe medical aid during war.

I am not sure if India has any doctrine for passive air defence and if our home ministry has any plans for damage manage from air attacks in case of war. India must build underground hospitals and medical aid posts. It has also built bomb-shelters for every locality.

Electronic Warfare

Electronic warfare like hacking networks, stealing, or collecting information, jamming etc. is commonplace. China, Israel and possible the US implants spying devices in all kinds of equipment supplied by them. Israel also managed to plant explosives in pagers supplied by Taiwan to Hezbollah and could detonate them to kill or injure thousands of Hezbollah commanders and fighters. There is the US Star Link celestial communication network, spy satellites and drones in the sky collecting information about vital installations and potential targets. Both Pakistan and Bangladesh have Star Link communication network. Battlefield communications are likely to be the first targets in any future war.

I sincerely hope that India is well prepare for cyber warfare and has contingency plans for communication of information, orders, and instruction if normal communications are disrupted.

Summary

Air force has three roles; air combat for control of the air over the battle field, interdiction or isolation of the battle field from rear areas and logistic support by destroying roads, railways, bridges etc. and close air support to ground troops. Ukraine does not have an air force worth its name. Hence, **Russian air force did not need fifth or sixth generation fighters for air combat roles. Missiles and drones proved to be more effective** means for interdiction and even close air support for ground troops.

Drones have played a dominant role in Ukraine war both for destruction of enemy energy infrastructure, interdiction, and close air support.

Russian battlefield surveillance has been a miserable failure. Its inability to detects Ukraine's preparations for Kursk offensive was unpardonable and cost it dearly. Ukraine, with NATO assistance has much better battlefield surveillance and target acquisition capability as demonstrated by sinking of Russian Flagship, the Markova.

Limitation of air defence systems against missiles and drones have been demonstrated both in Ukraine and Israel.

Israel has used **helicopters in anti-drone role** quite effectively.

Passive air defence systems like tunnels and underground shelters have proved effective against relentless Israeli air and drone attacks.

Israel has demonstrated the power of cyber warfare in degrading Hezbollah communication systems and caused large casualties.

Analysis

India's need for expensive fifth or sixth generation aircraft for air combat role is limited. Purchase of a few of these for half the defence budget for acquisition starves the others of funds. **What Indian air force needs are large numbers of new third generation fighters preferably indigenously made and lots of drones and air defence capability.**

India's capabilities of producing and using drones and its battlefield target acquisition system is not in public domain. **One can only hope that our armed forces have acquired adequate capability in this vital weapon system of modern warfare.**

A failure by India to detect assembly of large Chinese forces around Yadong and Doka La and Bangladesh's forces opposite Siliguri-Jalpaiguri could lead to loss of the Siliguri Corridor and subsequently the entire North East. **India needs to deploy satellite-based surveillance of Yadong-Dokalam and Northern Bangladesh.**

Israel has repeatedly used helicopters to shoot down long-range drones fired from Iran or Yemen. This use of helicopters in air defence role merits serious consideration.

It is not cost effective for India to go in for expensive imported air defence systems like S 500 except for air defence of Delhi and its air bases. India must go in for cheaper passive air defences like tunnels, underground facilities, and camouflage. I am not sure if India has any doctrine for passive air defence and if our home ministry has any plans for damage management caused by air attacks in case of war.

Electronic warfare like hacking networks, stealing, or collecting information, jamming etc. is commonplace. China, Israel and possible the US implants spying devices in all kinds of equipment supplied by them. **I sincerely hope that India is well prepare for cyber warfare and has contingency plans for communication of information, orders, and instruction if normal communications are disrupted.**

CHAPTER SIX

Indian Army: Strength and Weaknesses

I am making no comments on the Indian Air Force and Indian Navy as I do not have adequate knowledge of understanding of their strategies and tactics. My comments on the Indian Army are based on my experience of 28 years' service in the Indian Army from 1963 to 1991 and what I read in newspapers and internet and hear on the various television channels. These are my personal views. It is not necessary that all should agree with me. My aim will be achieved if my views are considered with an open mind and acted upon if they have any merit.

I would like to again emphasize that my comments are not directed at any person or political party but made in good faith and for the good of our great nation.

Strengths

Size. India Armed Forces are the third largest in terms of numbers.

Tradition of Valour. The history of the Indian Army is a tale of valour and sacrifice. This valour and sprit of sacrifice dates back thousands of years. In the olden days, there were more stories of glorious martyrdoms than glorious victories. That changed with the rigorous training and discipline in the British Indian Army. 16 lakh Indian soldiers fought in the World War I. Over 74,000 of them never returned alive. Over 20 lakhs fought in the World War II. Over 87,000 lost their lives. The valour and fighting spirit of the Indian Army was again on display in the 1947-48 Kashmir War. Indian Army not only stopped the raiders at the fringes of Srinagar at the Battle of Shalteng (Outstanding Victories of the Indian Army by the author) but defeated the Pakistan Army at the Battle of Zojila and the Battle of Rajouri. The period from 1948 to 1962 was a period of decline of the Indian Army's preparedness for war. The result was a humiliating defeat at the hands the Chinese in 1962. But even in the inglorious defeat, the tradition of valour and sacrifice was on display in many units. The humiliation made the government wake up and pay attention to making the Army prepared for battle. With the army at full strength and led from the front by junior officers, an out gunned Indian Army stopped the Pakistani Army at Khemkaran and Akhnoor and won an outstanding victory at Hajipir. The Indian Army's fighting capabilities and strategic acumen were on full display when the Indian Army routed the Pakistan Army in East Pakistan in a remarkable blitz in just 15 days. Indian peace keeping operations in Sri Lanka was an aimless exercise doomed to fail. It was a failure to set clear operational aims and not of valour or fighting spirit. The tradition of valour and ability to achieve victory was again on display during the Kargil War of 1999.

Junior Leadership. It is the junior leadership of the Indian Army that was behind the Indian Army's tradition of valour. They were with the men in war and peace. They trained together. They played games together. They ate and drank together at Barakhanas. The led from the front. A Pakistani soldier in a POW camp in Madhya Pradesh after the Bangladesh war when asked why they were defeated, they said that if they had officers like the Indian company and platoon commanders, they would have never lost. Today, junior officers are hard to find in fighting units, infantry battalions, armoured regiments, artillery regiments, engineer regiments and signal regiments. Once when attending an Infantry Day Dinner hosted by the local infantry brigade, I found that we were fifty-five guests and there were only seventeen infantry officers from the three infantry battalions and the brigade headquarters.

Weaknesses

I fear that the Army is in Pre-1962 State? There are signs of malice that plagued the Army before the 1962 debacle. There is a critical shortage of junior officers. All units are severely understaffed. Morale is low as seen from the number of suicides and fratricides that are taking place. I have no idea of what the equipment state is; whether there are adequate stocks of ammunition; whether any training takes place or the men are busy either manning the borders, fighting insurgents and doing spit and polish in the peace stations.

Shortage of Junior Officers.(Source: www.sansad.in **Digital Sansad, www.theprint.in>defense).** Almost 54 years have passed since 1971. There are signs of weaknesses that plagued the Army before the 1962 debacle.

There is a critical shortage of junior officers. All units are severely understaffed. Morale is low as seen from the number of suicides and fratricides that are taking place. **Currently, there is a shortfall of 7799 Officers in the Indian Army;** 1446 Officers in the Indian Navy; and 572 Officers in the Indian Air Force. The figure keeps changing. The entire shortage is about 15 to 20% of the authorized strength. The shortage is only in junior officers i.e. in the ranks of Lt. and Capt. The situation is aggravated by the officers being away on leave, courses, and temporary duties. The main drawbacks of the shortage are given below.

Destruction of Officer-jawan camaraderie. When were young officers and in full strength, we went for physical training or drill parade in the morning, and we played games with them in the evening. We chatted and drank with them at Barakhanas. We knew the men by name, their strengths, and weaknesses. These things do not happen anymore. The few officers available are busy all day with administrative duties. This officer-jawan bonding enabled the Indian Army to defeat the enemy in 1965, 1971, and the Kargil War.

Superseded Officers. When I commanded the regiment in 1980, two of my four company commanders were superseded majors. That was bad enough. Today, a Commanding Officer will have under them two to three time-scale Lt. Cols, senior to them in service. Only the Commanding Officers know the problems of motivating such officers to undertake hazardous missions.

Physical Fitness. With officers of the units sitting in office doing administrative duties all day long, they have no time to go for physical training and playing games. The number of officers over 40 have increased. Today's officers are mostly physically unfit for battle. The Commanding Officer today is more physically fit than many of his senior officers in the unit.

The problem of officer's shortage is not a new problem. It has existed since 1985 and is a direct fallout of the Armed Forces top Brass decision to accept shortages to ensure quicker promotions to colonels and above. The fact that the IAS and IPS officers reach brigadier or DIG rank with less service has always bugged them. The only solution they could think of is reduce intake of officers. After all, the code of senior officers of the armed forces is, **"There will be no war. If there is war, I will not be there to fight. So why not keep saying yes and keep furthering your career."** Promotions are more important than the interest of the nation.

There are two ways of having full complement of officers without stagnation of deserving officers for promotion. But first our generals must understand why the IAS and IPS officers get promoted to the rank of DIG ranks much faster. There are separate cadres for filling up officers in the lower ranks. In central services there is the Staff Selection Commission (SSC) entry. In the states there is the state administrative services like Rajasthan Administrative Services (RAS). **Army could adopt a new entry scheme** with relaxed Officer-Like Quality (OLQ) requirements for filling up the positions held by junior officers up to major.

The other option is to start a system of out of turn promotions for potential generals. In this system, deserving officers will be promoted to the rank of major at 4 years' service and Lt. Col. At 8 years' service and allotted a new seniority for promotion. To bring objectivity to the selection process, two competitive promotion examinations should be introduced; one for Captains and one for Majors. The subjects covered should be Indian Military History 1947-2000, modern weapon systems, foreign armies, and leadership. The selected captains should be put through the "Junior Command Course" and majors must have done DSSC and senior command courses. I would prefer this method as it focusses on producing more qualified generals.

Shortage of Soldiers in Fighting Units. (Source: www.sansad.in). In an answer to a question in the parliament, the government admitted that there was a shortage 108685 soldiers, 12151 sailors and 5217 airmen. This figure keeps changing with retirements and casualties, usually for the worse. About 50 thousand soldiers retire every year. There has been no recruitment of soldiers for two to three years. So, the actual shortage of soldiers could be over 200,000. To bureaucrats, politicians and even our senior officers the shortage is miniscule and does not affect fighting efficiency. **Any honest officer who has commanded a unit will tell you that this shortage seriously affects operational efficiency. Shortage of manpower means almost daily night duties, curtailment, and refusal of leave even in compassionate cases, and lack of training.** The first two seriously affect morale. In my 28 years' service, I do not recollect a single case of a jawan committing suicide. Today, about a hundred suicides take place every year. Lack of training seriously affects operational efficiency. Better training enabled the Indian Army to defeat a much better equipped Pakistani Army in 1965 War. **Normal recruitment of jawans under the old scheme must start now.** It takes one year to train a jawan in the regimental centre. It takes a year or more for a jawan to find his feet in the unit and to become an effective member of the fighting unit.

"Agniveer" Scheme. This is a new recruitment scheme introduced in place of the traditional one. Under the old scheme, soldiers were recruited for a minimum period of 17 years and were given a pension on retirement. This regular recruitment scheme has been discontinued. Agniveers are recruited on contract for four years. The recruits are given one year training at regimental centres and then posted to a battalion or regiment. Their services are terminated after four years. Twenty five percent are retained. The scheme has been introduced ostensibly to keep the armed forces young. The real motive is to save on payment of pensions. **The scheme is a disaster for the following reasons.**

Murder of Regimental Spirit. The main motivation for a soldier to be ready to sacrifice his life in war is the regimental spirit. Each battalion of the fighting arms has a long history of glory earned by acts of bravery and sacrifice recorded as honors like Param Vir Chakra and Battle Honors. This history motivates a soldier to give his best in battle. In addition, the soldiers in a regiment grow up together as a family. They join the army together, go through training at regimental centres together, eat together, play together, sleep together, train together, share dangers, joys and sorrows together. They are ready to sacrifice themselves for their comrades and their regiment's honour and glory. This spirit, which is the source of the legendary fighting spirit of the Indian Army, cannot be generated in three years in an Agniveer. It is this spirit which enabled a handful of Indian soldiers fight and defeat the Chinese who were three times more in numbers and well prepared with sticks and clubs at Ghalwan. This was the spirit that enabled Indian Army to retake the mountain peaks during the Kargil War. Without this spirit the Indian Army will never win another battle.

The Agniveer learns nothing about fighting. When the Agniveer joins a unit, everyone knows that he is a guest soldier. He will not be given any responsibility. He will be given fringe duties like cook-house assistant, ration collection duties, regimental police duties and the like. He will hardly get any opportunity for collective training which happens once a year and be a misfit in war. In the fourth year, he will be thinking of what he is going to do when he is discharged and not about his duties.

There is no appraisal system for jawans till they become non-commissioned officers. **Who will decide which Agniveer should be retained** and who should be discharged. Will the selection be based on caste, religion, state from which he comes or will money be paid for being retained.

Inadequate Spending on Defence. This started in 1991 when Mr. Manmohan Singh was finance minister. It was a condition for the IMF loan that was taken that India would not spend more than 3% of GDP on defence. That may be continuing. China has been spending 7% of GDP for years. China's GDP is also much larger than ours. Every year, we are falling behind China in the arms race.

Indigenous arms manufacturing capability. India has been the world's largest buyer of defence organizations in the country. Indigenous manufacturing was in the hands of the Ordnance Factories since British times. They were arguably the worst manufacturing organizations in India. Mercifully, Modiji has had them converted to defence PSUs in 2021. That by itself is not enough. These PSUs need adequate technology, working capitals and orders. Do they have access to technology, working capital and orders? It may be desirable to split Hindustan Aeronautics Limited into two or three PSUs to make it less top heavy and more efficient. Private Sector needs to be involved in defence production in a big way. Joint venture between defence PSUs, with surplus land and infrastructure and private sector firms with access to technology and expertise could speed up defence production.

Air Defence Capability. We see the destructive power of missiles and drones daily in the Ukraine War. Do we have adequate air defence capability?

Drones. Drones are an indispensable part of modern-day warfare. Do we have what we need?

Hardening of Defences. The destructive capabilities of modern multi-barrel artillery systems, missiles and drones is on full display in Ukraine-Russia War and the Israel-Hamas/Hezbollah War. Russia with all its air defence capabilities have not been able to stop Ukraine's drones and missiles from striking energy infrastructure, air fields and defence production units 800 km from the border. Hamas and Hezbollah are pounded day and night by Israeli air and drone strikes but have been able to preserve enough military manpower and hardware to keep fighting after 15 months of pounding. They have been able to do so because of the passive defence systems in the form of underground tunnels. Indian Airforce is unfit for war. I have no information about our air defence capabilities. In any case it is financially impossible to deploy air defence systems like Israeli Iron Dome for all vulnerable areas and points from the Pakistani Border in

Punjab to Arunachal Pradesh.

Summary

The main strengths of the Indian Army have been its fighting spirit and junior leadership. The main weaknesses of the Indian Army are summarized below.

Address Shortage of Junior Officers. Junior Officers, captains and lieutenants are the backbone of the Indian Army. The options for overcoming the stagnation problem have been explained above.

Abolish "Agniveer" recruitment of the combat arms like infantry, armoured Corps, Artillery, Corps of Engineers and Corps of Signals. The detailed reasons have been explained above.

Inadequate Spending on Defence. India must spend 5 to 7 percent of the GDP on defence if it wants to develop adequate deterrence.

Indigenous Weapon Production Capacity. We cannot continue to be worlds largest arms purchaser. Modiji has done a wonderful job by converting Ordnance Factories into Defence PSUs. But that is not enough. These PSUs must be given adequate funds and orders. Joint ventures with Private Sector should be established.

Air Defence Capability. We must indigenously develop effective air defence systems.

Drones. India must develop all the various types of drones use in modern warfare and produce them in adequate numbers indigenously.

Hardening of Defences. It is financially impossible for a large country like India to have air defence systems like the Israeli Iron Dome from Punjab to Arunachal. India must focus on passive air defence systems like underground tunnels and shelters.

Analysis

Indian political and military leadership have ignored the weaknesses of the Indian Armed Forces for most of our 78 years of independence. That has to change. Otherwise we could face a crushing defeat as we did in 1962.

CHAPTER SEVEN

Comparison of Capabilities Pakistan, China, Bangladesh and India

If you know the enemy and know yourself, you need not fear the result of a hundred battles. If you know yourself but not the enemy, for every victory gained you will also suffer a defeat. If you know neither the enemy nor yourself, you will succumb in every battle." · Sun Tzu · Art of War"

China

Chinese Intentions

All ambiguity about Chinese intentions of solving its border disputes with its neighbours is over. President Xi Jinping has passed a new border law that lays down how China is going to secure its borders. The new law has been in effect since January 1, 2022.

Law for Protection and exploitation of China's Land border Areas. The Standing Committee of the National People's Congress, China's top legislative body, passed a new law on October 23, 2021 laying down the law for "protection and exploitation of the country's land border areas". The law is not meant specifically for the border with India. China has about 22,500 km land boundary with 14 countries including India. The new Law has 62 articles and seven chapters. Some salient features are given in the succeeding paragraphs.

As per the law, the People's Republic of China shall set up boundary markers on all its land borders to clearly mark the border. The type of marker is to be decided in agreement with the neighbouring country in question. It will be clear that China is likely to dig in its heels at the current disputed positions at the LAC and will construct more dual-purpose model border villages which can be used both for military and civilian purposes. A number of these dual purpose villages have come up in Arunachal and Doklam.

The law further stated that People's Liberation Army (PLA) and Chinese People's Armed Police Force will maintain security along the border. This responsibility includes cooperating with local authorities in combating illegal border crossings.

The law prohibits any party from indulging in any activity in the border area which would "endanger national security or affect China's friendly relations with neighbouring countries". It includes construction of any permanent buildings by any person without authorisation from the concerned authority.

The Law further it states that citizens and local organisations are mandated to protect and defend the border infrastructure, maintain security and stability of borders and co-operate with government agencies in maintaining border security. The law lays down the path for the development of the border region. It states that People's Republic of China will take up education and propaganda to "solidify the sense of community of China, to promote the spirit of China, to defend the unity and territorial integrity of the country, strengthen citizens' sense of the country and homeland security, and build a common spiritual home for the Chinese nation" amongst citizens in the border region.

The Law permits the Chinese State to take measures "to strengthen border defence, support economic and social development as well as opening-up in border areas, improve public services and infrastructure in such areas, encourage and support people's life and work there, and promote coordination between border defence and social, economic development in border areas". In other words, the encourages the Chinese Government to settle civilians in the border areas and thereby consolidate territorial claims.

The new land border law is a clear attempt by China to unilaterally delineate and demarcate territorial boundaries with India and Bhutan. The territorial disputes are now non-negotiable. India, Nepal, Bhutan and other countries will have to accept Chinese claims or be ready to fight. As a follow up of the law, China renamed 15 places of Arunachal Pradesh in their map on December 30, 2021. The Law paves the way for enabling China to take over illegal control of sovereign territories of other countries.

Analysis

The Indian people and the Indian Government need to understand and accept that all military and diplomatic discussions with the Chinese about territorial disputes with China are useless.It is Chinese solution or no solution. Any statement by a Chinese politician or diplomat saying that its relations with India is improving is only intended to lull India into a state of complacency which is to be exploited at the time of Its choosing. Just as India keeps saying that only issue remaining with Pakistan is liberation of POK, China must also be telling its people that the only remaining issue with India is liberation of Arunachal. India must either give in to Chinese demands or get ready to fight. It will be naïve to think that China will immediately launch attacks to take territories they claim. They will use threats and propaganda to encourage its enemies to give up without a fight. The Authorhopes that Indian Government will not surrender without a fight and that **"India is ready for battle."**

Chinese Armed Forces

China's armed forces are ranked the largest in the world with a combined strength of about 2.2 million men at arms and about one million reserves. It had a military budget of US $209 in 2020, which is second only to the US. India in comparison had a budget of only about US $ 54 billion 2021-22.

Regular Army

In the last twenty years it has gone all out to modernize its forces. The regular army has been reduced by about 500,000 men over the past few years with the 500,000 being transferred to Armed Police Divisions which have been deployed on its borders. Combat effectiveness is sought to be increased by technology-intensive elements such as special forces, army aviation (transport aircraft and helicopters), surface to air missiles (SAM) and electronic warfare units. The latest operational doctrine of the PLA ground forces highlights the importance of information technology, electronic and cyber warfare and long-range precision missile strikes in future wars. The older generation command, control, and communications (C3) systems are being replaced by an integrated battlefield information networks featuring local/wide-area networks (LAN/WAN), satellite communications, unmanned aerial vehicle (drone) based surveillance and reconnaissance systems and mobile command and control centres. Russia exports latest technology and weapons systems to China. However, modernization of a large force as that of China requires time and money. So, the Chinese formations are classified as Category A or Category B. Category

A formations have priority for modernization.

Combined Arms Brigades

The Chinese Armed Forces have been reorganized in 2016/2017. Their basic fighting formation is a Combined Arms Brigade in line with the US Army. (**Source: reditt.com/r/AustralianMiliyary /comments /10m9sb8/ Chinese_Combined_ Arms_Brigades_Overview/?rdt=34006.**)

The Chinese have discarded big infantry or armoured divisions and adopted a system of all-round brigades that can be given different tasks. By deleting a layer of mid-level organisation (the division), they have taken command and control away from their weaker mid-level commanders, emphasising junior and senior command. This is a Western style of command and control used in NATO forces.

There are three main Combined Arms Brigades (CABs), the Heavy, Medium, and Light. They are organised under Chinese Group Armies. Each Group Army has about six CABs within it. Heavy CABs have an emphasis on tanks and armour, whereas light CABs are focused on dismounted infantry ops. There is also a fourth type of CAB- the Amphibious Combined Arms Brigades.

Each Brigade has four Combined Arms Battalions. The composition of the battalions will differ depending on the type of CAB. Each battalion will have four companies and one Firepower Coy (mortars and anti-tank weapons). Each brigade also has a Service Support Battalion (including battalion's recon and engineer platoons), a Reconnaissance Battalion, an Artillery Battalion, an Air Defence Battalion, an Operational Support Battalion (Command and Control, EW, NBC defence, BDE level engineer equipment, etc) and a Service Support Battalion (Supply, medical, maintenance).

A heavy combined arms battalions consist of battalions HQ company (including medical, reconnaissance, and air defence platoon, four combat companies including two tank companies (14 tanks per company), and two mechanized infantry companies (14 armoured personnel carriers per company), one firepower company, and one combat support company.

Border Defence Regiment

A Border Defence Regiment consists of the Regiment HQ, three battalions of three companies each. (Source: jjamwal.in/yayavar / Chinese-armed-force-part-3-ground forces/8/). The strength of each regiment is about 2800. Thus each Border Defence Regiment is almost equal to our brigade, the difference being our brigades have three battalions of four companies.

Chinese Army Structure. This section should be studied with a Google Map of China on a laptop by those who understand military strategy and tactics.

The Chinese Army is organized into five theatre commands.

Eastern Theatre Command. Its' area of responsibility includes East China, the East China Sea and the Taiwan Strait. The command's primary missions are maintaining security in the East China Sea and the conduct of major operations against Taiwan.

Southern Theatre Command. Its area of responsibility includes Mynmar, Laos, Vietnam, mainland South East Asia and the South China Sea. The command's primary missions are maintaining security in the South China Sea and includes supporting the Eastern Theatre Command in any major operation against Taiwan.

Central Theatre Command. The command's primary responsibility is the defence of capital, Beijing, and it serves as the national strategic military reserve

Northern Theatre Command. Its primary responsibility is the Russian and Mongolian borders.

Western Theatre Command. Its jurisdiction includes Sichuan, Tibet, Gansu, Ningxia, Qinghai, Xinjian, Shaanxi, Yunan, and Chongqing and Guizhou. The entire LA C is the responsibility of this Command. Its Area of Responsibility consists of India, South Asia, Central Asia, Western Mongolia. Its headquarters is in Lanzhou in Gansu District. This Command has the 76th Group Army, the 77th Group Army and the Tibet Military Region. (Source: jjamwal.in/yayavar / Chinese-armed-force-part-3-ground forces/8/).

76th **Group Army**, HQ Xining, Qinghai. it consists of six CABs, 12th Heavy Combined Arms Brigade located in Jiquan, Gansu; 17th Heavy Combined Arms Brigade, 56th Light Combined Arms Brigade, 62nd Heavy Combined Arms Brigade; 149 Heavy Combined Arms Brigade, 182 Light Combined Arms Brigade. In addition it has 76th Special Operations Brigade, 76th Army Aviation Brigade, 76th Artillery Brigade, 76th Air Defense Brigade, 76th Engineering and Chemical Defense Brigade and 76th Service Support Brigade.

77th **Group Army.** Chongzhou, Chengdu, Sichwan. It consists of six CABs, 39th Heavy Combined Arms Brigade; 40th Mountain Combined; 55th Light Combined Arms Brigade, 139 Heavy Combined Arms Brigade, 150

Mountain Combined Arms Brigade and 181 Medium Combined Arms Brigade. In addition it has 77th Special Operations Brigade, 77th Army Aviation Brigade – Operates MI-17 helicopters; 77th Artillery Brigade; 77th Air Defence Brigade, 77th Engineering Brigade, 77th Chemical Defence Brigade and 7reorganization of the Chinese 7th Service Support Brigade.

Other units under Western Theatre Command are Third Brigade of Reconnaissance Intelligence, third Brigade of Information Support, third Brigade of Electronic Warfare, 53 Mountain Motorized Infantry Brigade and 54th Brigade.

Tibet Military District

The Tibet Military District has been in existence since 1956. In the 2016-17 reorganization of the Chinese Army, the Military District was elevatelistedd to a sub-Theatre Grade Command directly under the Army HQ and only administratively under Western Theatre Command. It is commanded by a Lt. Gen. and its HQ is located at Lhasa.

(Source: en.wikipedia.org/wiki/Tibet_Military_District, jjamwal.in/ yayavar / Chinese-armed-force-part-3-ground forces/8/).

Subordinate Units of Tibet Military District are 52 Mountain Combined Arms Brigade, Linzi City, Sighaste; 53 Mountain Combined Arms Brigade, Zedang, Nedong County, Shannan prefecture; 54 Mountain Combined Arms Brigade, Dongga Bridge, Lhasa; 85th Special Operation Brigade, ; 85th Army Aviation Brigade; 85th Artillery Brigade; 85th Air-Defence Brigade; 85th Engineering and Chemical Brigade; 7th Electronic Countermeasures Brigade; 5th Motorized Transport Brigade; Tibet Military Region Communication Regiment. Tibet Military District has thirteen to fourteen Border Guard Regiments; 351st Border Guard Regiment, Zayu County, Nyingchi prefecture; 352nd Border Guard Regiment, Medog County, Nyingchi Prefecture; 353rd Border Guard Regiment, Mainling City, Nyingchi Prefecture; 354th Border Guard Regiment, Lhunze County, Lhoka Prefecture; 355th Border Guard Regiment, Cona County, Lhoka Prefecture; 356th Border Guard Regiment, Yadong County, Shigatse Prefecture: 357th Border Guard Regiment, Tingri County, Shigaste Prefecture and 358th Border Guard Regiment, Saga County, Shigatse Prefecture; 1 Border Guard Regiment, Shannan City, Longzi County, 2 Border Guard Regiment, Cuona County; 3rd Border Guards Regiment, Shigaste, Tingri County; 4th Border Regiment, Chyau, Linzhi County; 5th Border Regiment, Saga County; 6th Border Regiment, Yadong County, .

The Ngari Prefecture which borders Ladakh, Himachal and Uttarakhand comes under Xinjiang Military District.

Xinjiang Military District

Source: en.wikipedia.org/wiki/Xinjiang_Military_District

The Xinjiang Military District has similar status as Tibet Military District as Deputy Theatre Grade and is directly under the Central Military Commission. The district includes all of Xinjiang and Ngari District of Tibet. It is in charge of the disputed area of Aksai Chin and the LAC in Ladakh. It has been in a a protracted stand-off with India Army since 2020. Xinjiang is one of the few military regions in which full divisions are still retained as an organizational level post the 2016-17 reorganization of the Chinese Armed Forces. It has fifteen Border Defence regiments assigned as well as the main fighting force.

The units and formation under the Xinjiang are 4 Combined Arms Division, Kucha City, Aksu Prefecture; 6 Combined Arms Division, Kasgar; 8 Combined Arms Division, Wushu, Khazak Prefecture; 11 Combined Arms Division, Urumqi; 84 Special Forces Brigade, Kasgarh; 84 Army Aviation Brigade, Changi; 84 Artillery Brigade, Urumqi, 84 Air Defence Brigade, Urumqi; 6 intelligence and Surveillance Brigade, Urumqi; 6 Information Support Brigade, Urumqi; 6 Electronic Countermeasure Brigade, Urumqi; 4 motorized Transport Brigade, 3 Motorized Transport Regiment, 1st Communication Regiment, 2nd Communication Regiment, 2nd Chemical Defence Regiment, 9th Combat Engineer Regiment and Construction Engineer Regiment, Rutog, Ngari Prefecture. Of the fifteen border defence regiments, two are located in Ngari Prefecture; 361 Border Defence Regiment, Tsamda County and 362 Border Defence Regiment, Rutog. 363 Border Defence Regiment Located at Sahidulla, Pishan County, Hotan Prefecture and the 362 Border Defence Regiment were engaged in the fighting with India Army at Galwan and Pangan Tso in 2020.

Equipment

The priority CABs of the Chinese Army are very well equipped with the la wetest equipment. The Chinese

PLA's Fighting Prowess

The Korean War was the first war fought by China after independence. In 1950, the PLA attacked the US forces in the Korean Peninsula in support of North Korea. At this stage, the PLA was battle hardened due to China's long conflict with Japanese occupation, World War II and civil war with Nationalists. The PLA suffered heavy casualties but fought the technologically superior US armed forces, who had total air superiority, with skill and determination and brought them to a standstill.

The Sino Indian conflict of 1962 was the next war PLA fought. In October 1962, the PLA routed the Indian Army in Ladakh and Arunachal and declared unilateral ceasefire after taking possession of over 30,000 sq. km of Indian territory in about a month of fighting. **The Chinese success was largely due to the total unpreparedness of the Indian Army and exceptionally poor Indian military leadership. It was also due to a total failure of the political leadership of India and government of India to assess correctly the PLA's capabilities and intentions and to build a professional well equipped armed forces that could defend its borders.**

The Sino-Vietnam War of 1979 was the last major Military adventure of the PLA. China wanted "to teach a lesson" to the Vietnamese for their attack on Khmer Rouge in Cambodia in 1978. On 17 February 1979, a PLA force of about 200,000 troops supported by 200 tanks entered northern Vietnam. The initial PLA attack soon lost its momentum. A new attack wave was launched with eight divisions. On 6 March, China declared that their punitive mission had been achieved. The PLA crossed the border back into China on 16 March. Both sides declared victory.

Present-day Troop Quality

(Source: reditt.com/r/AustralianMilitary/comments /10m9sb8/ Chinese_Combined _ Arms_ Brigades _ Overview/ ?rdt=34006.)

The Chinese soldiers are conscript soldiers. All males in China in the age bracket of 18-22 must register for military service. Not all are taken. Conscripts are selected from volunteers. **Conscripts serve for three years in the Army and 4 years in the navy and air force. This short tenure is not enough for collective training at section, platoon, company and battalion level. Building regimental spirit or bonding which is the primary motivation for infantry, armoured corps and engineers who must fight enemy troops at close quarters is completely missing. Fear of punishment is the only motivation for fighting. Chinese soldiers have never been fired at by artillery, air craft or even small arms since 1979 when they fought the Vietnamese. No one knows how they will react when they come under fire and have to pick up the dead and the wounded.** China has never fought a war since 1979 when they attempted a punitive expedition in Vietnam where they were soundly defeated. **Chinese commanders have no war experience.** The Chinese CABs are reportedly comprised of a large amount of contract troops. A substantial part of training is done at unit level. The Chinese has another new intake of troops Every six months. It takes them about six months to give them basic training. So, their CABs have a large number of untrained soldiers. The Chinese soldiers are also only sons. As was seen at Galwan and Pang Tso, Indian soldiers, particularly the Infantry, are better trained and motivated. They have also been under fire while fighting terrorists in Kashmir.

Analysis

Chinese Army is very large. Its elements on the LAC and opposite Taiwan are likely to be well equipped with state of art equipment. However, China has not fought any major battle since its misadventure against Vietnam in 1979. The Chinese soldier is also an only son and a contract soldier. His fighting capabilities have not been tested. The tactical and strategic acumen of its generals are unknown. The Chinese soldiers are not supermen. **But the Chinese army has the edge in numbers and technology and their capabilities must not be under estimated.**

Chinese Air Force

The Chinese Air Force was reorganized in 2016-17. It now has fivetheatre commands with same areas of responsibility as the army commands. According to International Institute for Strategic Studies, the Chinese Air Force introduced over 600 fourth and fifth generation fighters between 2016 and 2022. It is accepted as a strategic air force with the capabilities of conducting global operations to protect Chinese interests. India has to deal with the Western Air Force Theatre Command which has responsibility in Tibet and Xinjiang Regions.

The Chinese Air Force is now organized as air force divisions. Each air division has a number of air brigades. Each air brigade has two to three air regiments. Each air Regiment has two to three air groups and 16 to 30 aircraft. Each group has two to three air squadrons and 8 to 10 aircraft. Each squadron has 2 to 4 aircraft. **Source: cenjows.in>wp-content>uploads>2023 PDF**

Chinese Air Force in Tibet

Chinese Air Force has significantly increased its presence in Tibet. It has deployed advanced fighter jets like the J-20, and has expanded its airbase infrastructure, including the construction of new airfields and upgrades to existing ones.

Airbase Expansion and Modernization. China has constructed numerous airbases in Tibet, including those at Hoping, Pangta, Shiquanhe, Bayixincun, and Kong Ka. Several airfields, at Lhasa, Shannan, and Xigaze, have been upgraded and expanded, with many runways reaching 4,000 meters in length. China has also built new heliports and upgraded existing ones. Airfields in Xinjiang, such as Hotan, have also been upgraded.

Deployment of Advanced Aircraft. The Chinese Air Torce has deployed its fifth-generation stealth fighter, the J-20, at airbases in Tibet, including Shigatse. Other fighter jets, such as the J-7, J-8, J-10, J-11, and J-16, have also been deployed in Tibetan airfields. The PLAAF has also deployed KJ-500, an early warning airborne and control system, as well as helicopters and drones.

Air Defence. China has also been upgrading its surface-to-air missile complexes in the region.

Deployment

The Chinese have three main air force bases in Tibet; at Lhasa Gonggar Airport, Xianguanying Air Base Lanzhou,and Urumqi air base at Urumqi.

6th Fighter Division at Lanzhou. This division has seven air brigades. Each brigade has 30 to 50 fighters. Thus the division has 210 to 350 combat aircraft. **16 Air Brigade,** based at Ningxia, Yinchuan, Xihuayuan airbases and equipped with J 11B aircraft. **18 Air Brigade,** based at Gansu, Dinxi and Lintao Air base and equipped with J 10C fighters. **97 Air Brigade** at Chongqing, Dazu, withDengyunqiao air bases equipped with J 20A fighters, **98 Air Brigade** at Chongqing and Baishiyi Air bases equipped with J 16 fighters. 99 Air Brigade at Xinjiang, Hotan air bases equipped with J 16 fighters. **109 Air Brigade** at Xinjiang, Changji, air bases equipped with J 11A fighters; **110 Air Brigade** at Xinjiang, Urumqi and Nanshan Air base and equipped with JH 7A fighters. **111 Air Brigade** at Xinjiang and Golmud air bases equipped with J 20A fighters.

Transport Units of 4th Transport Division. Four air Regiments of this division are for Western Theatre Command. 10th Air Regiment located at Qionglai, Sichuan is equipped with Y-9 airchraft; 11th Air Regiment is located at Luzhou, Sichuan is equipped with Y-9 aircraft; 12th Air Regiment is located at Qionglai, Sichuan and equipped with Y-20 aircraft.

Tibet Military Region also has 85th Army Aviation Brigade.

Analysis

Chinese Air Force is the second-largest air force globally, with over 2,000 combat aircraft, including modern fighters like the J-20 stealth fighter and Su-35s. Iy has a larger fleet of airborne warning and control system (AWACS) aircraft, aerial tankers, and combat drones. It has a significant technological edge and a large indigenous development and manufacturing capability. China has two fifth generation fighter aircraft.

Indian Air Force is the fourth-largest globally with a fleet of about 900 aircraft. It has a few state of art fighters like Rafale and Su-30 MKI, it lags behind in indigenous development and production of advanced combat platforms. The IAF is known for its well-trained and motivated pilots with combat experience. The IAF is struggling to maintain its fighter squadron strength, with modernization efforts hampered by delayed deliveries, limited budget and limited indigenous development and production capability.

Chinese Air Force is much stronger than India's and the gap is going to widen every year because the Chinese defence budget is three times that of India. **India must pay attention to passive ait defence and shift all important operational and logistic installation under ground.**

Strategic Missile Forces

Sources: en.wikipedia.org/wiki/ Peoples_Liberation_Army_Rocket_Force

The Chinese Army's Rocket Force controls China's arsenal of land-based ballistic, hypersonic, cruise missiles Theatre, both nuclear and conventional. The Rocket Force comprises approximately 300,000 personnel and six ballistic missile "Bases" and three support Bases in charge of storage, engineering, and training respectively. The six operational Bases are independently deployed in the five Theatre Commands. Each Base controls a number of Rocket Brigades.

China has the largest land-based missile arsenal in the world. According to the US Department of Defence Estimates Chinese missile arsenal includes 400 ground-launched cruise missiles, 900 conventionally armed short-range ballistic missiles, 1,300 conventional medium-range ballistic missiles, 500 intermediate-range conventional ballistic missiles, and 400 intercontinental ballistic missiles. Many of these are precision guided, which would allow them to destroy targets even without nuclear warheads. It is said that China has a stockpile of approximately 500 nuclear warheads in 2023.

The 64th Missle Base is located within Western Theatre Command. Its HQ is at Lanzhou, Gansu. It has nine missile brigades. 641 Missile Brigade is located at Hancheng, Saanxi It has DF31 and DF 31AG missiles. 642 Missile Brigade is located at Datong, Saanxi and has DF 31AG missiles. 643 Missile Brigade is located at Tiangsu, Gansu and has DF31AG missiles. 644 Missile Brigade is located at Hanzhong, Saanxi and has DF41 missiles. 645 Missile

Brigade is located at Yinchuang, Xinxia DF41 missiles. 646 Missile Brigade is located at Korla, Xinjiang, DF21 and DF 26 missiles. 647 Missile Brigade at Zangye, Qinghai, is under construction. A new Missile Brigade is coming up atat Hami, Xinjiang. It has 120 silos. Another new Missile Brigade is coming up at Yumen, Gansu. It has 110 silos.

Analysis

China is well ahead of India in strategic missile forces. India has developed some strategic missiles. But it not clear if these missiles are operational and available in sufficient numbers to pose a deterrence. India also needs to develop anti-missile defence system and acquire them in adequate numbers to protect our air fields, refineries, and other critical targets. India must also focus on moving operational and logistic installations under-ground. It must also have adequate firefighting and rescue resouces which can be deployed at the time of war.

Chinese Drone Capability

Source: idsa.in/publisher/comments/chinas-increasing-global-drone-footprint. En.wikipedia.org/wiki /List-of-unmanned-aerial-vehicles-of-China . militarydrones.org.cn

Chinese military drones can be classified into reconnaissance drones, decoy drones, electronic countermeasures drones, communications relay drones, unmanned fighter drones and target aircraft. **Reconnaissance drones** are for artillery positioning and range reconnaissance. Reconnaissance drone is specially used to carry out reconnaissance from the air and gather intelligence and is one of the main reconnaissance tools in modern warfare. These drones are also used for battlefield surveillance and combat damage assessment. The main purpose of the **decoy drone** is to simulate the flight path of fighter aircraft, cruise missiles and radar signal characteristics to create false air condition, to induce the enemy radar to start up, to induce the enemy's air defence weapons to carry out attacks, to cover our penetration combat aircraft, and to cooperate with the electronic reconnaissance and anti-radiation attack forces to carry out combat tasks. At the same time, the mission system has the ability to jam the ground radar, and can provide effective training and evaluation means for radar and air defence forces in the complex electromagnetic environment. **Electronic countermeasures drone**, electronic countermeasures is a variety of electronic measures and actions taken by both sides to weaken and destroy the effectiveness of the other side's electronic equipment and ensure the effectiveness of their own electronic equipment, also known as electronic warfare. Airborne electronic countermeasure system is the main means of modern electronic countermeasure. With the development of ballistic missiles and satellites, outer space is a new battlefield, and electronic countermeasures will play an important role in the future modern warfare. **Communication relay drones.** In future wars, communications systems will be the lifeblood of battlefield command and control and the focus of attacks by both sides. drones communication network can establish a strong redundant backup communication link to improve the survivability. After being attacked, the backup communication network can recover quickly and play an irreplaceable role in network-based warfare. High-altitude, long-endurance drones extend the communication range, use satellites to provide alternative links, direct to land-based terminals, and reduce the threat of physical attack and noise interference. The **combat communication drones** adopt a variety of data transmission systems, and the in-line-of-sight simulation data transmission system is used among each combat unit. **Attack Drones** carry warheads or missiles and can suppress enemy air defence system, attack the ground forces, and attacking energy infrastructure, weapon depots etc. in depth areas. **Target Drones** are used as a target for shooting training for pilots and air defence systems.

China has established the world' largest Unmanned Aerial Vehicle (UAV or drone) industry. It has become the world's largest exporter of military drones. It exports drones to the UAE, Saudi Arabia, Egypt and Pakistan.

China has a number of drones in service with the Chinese Rocket Force, ChineseArmy, PLA Air Force and PLA Navy. The Chinese Air Force's drone brigade uses the Wing Loong-2 (GJ-2) drone, and the Chinese Army uses Rainbow-4 reconnaissance and strike drone. It is also using KVD002 medium-altitude long-flight reconnaissance and strike drone at the theatre command and group army levels.

The TB-001 drone is used for reconnaissance and as an attack drone. It is also used by Chinese Rocket Force's anti-ship ballistic missiles. China also uses drones for patrolling its land borders as well as coastlines, and particularly along the Sino-Indian border and Taiwan Strait.

Chinese drones have been deployed in large numbers in the Western Theatre Command. At present, PLA has deployed 'GJ-2' drones and 'Rainbow-4' drones in the Western Theatre Command for reconnaissance activities along the borders. The unmanned AV500W reconnaissance and strike integrated helicopter has been deployed on the Tibetan plateau. This unmanned helicopter weighs 450 kilograms and has a ceiling of 6,700 meters. It can carry four small laser-guided air-to-surface missiles to accurately strike enemy personnel and light vehicles.

Analysis

China is well ahead of India in production of indigenous drones and using them on the battle field'

Cyber Warfare Capability

Chinese cyber warfare is meant to disable the opponent's communication systems. China has rapidly developed its cyber warfare capability. China's military hackers defaced India's Defence Ministry and Bhaba Atomic Research Centre (BARC) Websites. Although no real damage was done, these are precursors. Chinese hackers have also occasionally hacked into Pentagon and White House computer systems. Recently, a cyber-attack, possibly by North Koreans, disabled many computer networks in the US and South Korea for almost one week.

Analysis

China appears to be ahead of India in terms of Cyber Warfare Capability. Not much is known about our cyber warfare capabilities.

Pakistan

Pakistan Army

(Source: globalsecurity.com, en.wikipedia.org/wiki/ Pakistan_Armed_Force). This section should be studied with a Google Map of Pakistan on a laptop by those who understand military strategy and tactics.

In 2024, the Pakistan Armed Forces had approximately 660,000 active personnel, excluding 25,000+ personnel in the Strategic Plans Division Forces, a paramilitary force in charge of Nuclear assets, and 291,000 active personnel in the various paramilitary forces. The Pakistan Army also runs a wide range of corporate/ commercial organization like the Fauji Foundation and Askati Bank.

Pakistan Army has a total of eight corps consisting of two armoured divisions, four mechanized divisions, fifteen infantry divisions and two artillery division. one Special Security Division, one division-sized formation called Northern Areas Command (operates in POK), and one engineer division. and three artillery divisions.

The Pakistan Army is divided into five military regions, Punjab, Sindh, J&K FANA, NWFP & FATA and Baluchistan.

Punjab Military Region. This region is responsible for Pakistan's border with Punjab, Haryana, and the northern part of Rajasthan. It holds all

Pakistan's offensive forces which consist of I Corps and II Corps. I Corp located at Mangla is composed of 6 Armoured Division (Kharian), 17 Mechanized Division (Kharian) and 37 Mechanized Division (Gurjanwala). II Corps located at Multan is composed of 1 Armoured Division (Multan), 14 Infantry Division (Okhra) and 40 Infantry Division (Okhra). The military region has three holding corps or defensive corps as given below. A holding corps is supposed to be capable of launching limited offensives, spoiling attacks, or diversionary attacks. IV Corp located at Lahore is composed of 10 Infantry Division and 11 Infantry Division, both located at Lahore. XXX Corps located at Gujranwala with 8 Infantry Division and 15 Infantry Division both located at Sialkot. XXXI Corps is located at Bhawalpur with 25 Mechanized Division and 35 Infantry Division both located at Bhawalpur.

Sindh Military Region. This region is responsible for Pakistan's borders with southern Rajasthan and Gujrat. It has only one corps the V Corps located at Karachi. V Corps is composed of 16 Infantry Division and 18 Infantry Division at Hyderabad and 35 Mechanized Division at Malir.

J&K and FANA Military Region. This military region is responsible for Pakistan's Line of Control in Jammu and Kashmir and Ladakh. There is only one corps in the region, X Corps located at Rawalpindi. The corps consists of Northern Area Command (POK), 12 Infantry Division (Muree), 19 Infantry Division (Jhelum/Rawalkot) and 23 Infantry Division at Mangla.

NWFP / FATA Military Region. This military region is responsible for Pakistan's borders with eastern Afghanistan. It is fighting Tahreek-e-Taliban and Al Qaeda. The region has one Corps the XI Corps located at Peshawar. It has 7 Infantry Division located at Mardan and 9 Infantry Division at Kohat.

Baluchistan Military Region. This military region is responsible for Pakistan's borders with southern Afghanistan and Iran. Pakistan is fighting a separatist insurgency in the region. The region has only one Corps, the XII Corps located at Quetta. It has two infantry divisions, 33 Infantry Division and 41 Infantry Division at Hyderabad (Sindh).

Pakistan Air Force

The Pakistan Air Force has its headquarters is in Rawalpindi. The air force is organized into eighteen (fifteen according to some sources) squadrons, with a total of about 400 combat aircraft. Its interceptors or air defense aircraft includes Chinese J-10s and J-7s. In ground-attack role they have Chinese JF-17, Mirage IIIs and Mirage Vs, one squadron of which is equipped with Exocet anti-ship missiles and deployed in an anti-ship role. Pakistan also has about 60 F-16s. The assembly of JF-17 aircrafts in Pakistan has commenced and eight to ten aircrafts will be assembled per year. Pakistan is also reported to be acquiring up to eight Erieye airborne surveillance system mounted on Saab 2000 aircraft of Sweeden. Pakistan is reported to have placed an order for the Chinese AWACS system ZDK-03 based on Chinese Y-8 aircraft. Pakistan has purchased 50 Mirage IIIs and Vs, 150 sealed pack engines and a huge quantity of Mirage spares from Libya. The Mirage Rebuild Factory, which is a part of PAC, had been rebuilding the 35-year-old version of the Mirage aircraft which were bought as scrap from various countries. The PAF is acquiring 2 Squadrons of the Italian Falco UAV. Eventually, the PAF plans to field 5-6 UAV Squadrons. The backbone of the transport fleet is twelve C-130 Hercules. To enable Pakistan to fight Taliban and Al Qaeda, the United States has delivered some refurbished C-130E transports, refurbished P-3C surveillance aircraft, refurbished Cobra helicopters, new Bell 412 helicopters and a number of Harpoon missiles, AN/TPS-77 surveillance radars, night vision goggles and AIM-9M Sidewinder missiles. The equipment will be used against India if required. Pakistan has also purchased some MI-171 helicopters from Ukraine for its Special Services Group (SSG). Pakistan has purchased four CN-235 air craft from Indonesia for VIP travel.

Analysis

Indian has a slight edge over Pakistan in air force capability. Indian pilots are also reputed to be better trained and more capable in air combat than Pakistani forces. But neither country can achieve complete control of the air and both air forces can cause considerable damage to the other, the ground forces and civilian infrastructure during wars.

Pakistani Army Aviation Corps

The Pakistani Army Aviation Corps operates about 350 aircraft, including approximately 40 AH-1 Cobra combat helicopters.

Pakistani Army Strategic Forces Command

The Pakistan Army Strategic Forces Command operates a wide rand range of missile systems. Its headquarters is at Chaklala near Rawalpindi. The Strategic Forces Command controls the land-based ballistic and cruise missile systems, both nuclear and conventional.

Analysis

India enjoys a slight superiority in both holding and offensive formations. The border between the two countries in Punjab and the lower reaches of Kashmir have well prepared permanent defenses, anti-tank ditches and defense-oriented canals and are defended in strength. It is unlikely that either side can make any major breakthrough in these sectors. Neither side could penetrate more than 15 to 20 km during 1965 and 1971 wars. **Those who keep advocating that India should attack Pakistan if it continues to support terrorism need to study the above figures and be acquainted with the reality.** Pakistan is well aware of its limitations in a conventional war with India. That is why Late President Zia ul Haq initiated his strategy of "Bleeding India from a Thousand Cuts" through Pakistan sponsored terrorism in Kashmir and North Eastern India. Economic constraints will make it difficult for Pakistan to fight a conventional war with India. However, in case of a war with China, it could activate our Western Front to tie down troops and prevent them from being redeployed to the east.

Bangla Desh

(Source: en.wikipedia.org/wiki/Bangladesh_Army)

Bangla Desh Army

Bangladesh Army was reorganized after liberation from Pakistan. The India friendly Awami League government under Sheikh Mujibur Rehaman was overthrown in 1975. General Zia Ur Rehman took over. The Bangladesh Government became anti India and pro-Pakistan/China. General Ershad assumed power in 1982. Starting in 1985, the army had experienced another spurt in growth assisted by China and Pakistan. Beginning in 2017, Bangla Desh Army embarked on a long-term modernization and reorganization. The force is being divided into three corps — Central, Eastern and Western. Three new infantry divisions have been raised, the 17 Infantry Division at Sylhet, 10 Infantry Division at Cox Bazar and 7 Infantry Division at Barishal-Patuakhali. This brought the strength of the Bangla Desh Army to ten divisions. It will not be out of place to mention that East Pakistan had only three infantry location. This was increased to four in 1970 when independence movement started. Bangladesh has borders with India and Myanmar.

Bangla Desh Army is being modernized and strengthened. Two commando battalions have been raised for special operations. Armoured units received the Chinese MBT-2000 in 2011, while the existing Type 69 MBT fleet has been upgraded. 174 Type 59 tanks are also being upgraded. Some 300 BTR-80 armoured personnel carriers and some Otoka TR-80r Cobra Light Assault vehicles and support vehicles have been introduced.

The artillery has been modernized with Nora B-52 K2 self-propelled artillery system FROM Serbia. Two regiments of WS-22 Guided Multiple Rocket Launcher System nave been raised. Anti-tank capabilities have been enhanced with Metis-M and PF-98 rocket systems. Two regiments of FM 90 surface to air missiles have been added to enhance air defence capabilities. The Army Aviation Wing is also being modernized. Bangladesh Army also procured 36 battlefield reconnaissance drones from Slovenia.

There has been a thaw in ties between Pakistan and Bangladesh after ousting of Sheikh Hasina. Chief of Army Staff Pakistan met General Asim Munir meets Lieutenant General S M Kamrul Hassan, principal staff officer of the Armed Forces Division of Bangladesh, at General Headquarters, Rawalpindi on 15 January 2025. They stressed the need for "enduring partnership" between the two countries.
(www.defese.pk/threads/
pakistan_bangladesh_underscore_enduring_partnership........).

Bangladesh Air Force

Bangla Desh Air Force has 17,390 personnel and 216 aircraft. These include Yakovlev Yak-130, Chengdu F-7 and MIG 29 fighters, Bell 212, Mi 17 and AW139 helicopters, C130 and An32 transport aircraft and a variety of trainers.

Location of Bangladesh Army Formations

(Source www.en.wikipedia.org/wiki/location_of_the_formations_of Bangladesh Army). This section should be studied with a Google Map of Bangladesh on a laptop by those who understand military strategy and tactics.

Bangladesh can be geographically divided into four regions, **Savar or Dhaka Region.** 9 Infantry Division is located here. The division consists of 12 Bengal Lancer Regiment, 5th Bangladesh Infantry Regiment, 9th Artillery Brigade, 71 Mechanized Infantry Brigade, 81st Infantry Brigade. 99 Composite brigade of the Division is located at Munshiganj.

Western Bangladesh or area south of River Padma up to the Bay of Bengal. This area borders West Bengal from Farraka to Sunder Ban. The main towns are Kushtia, Jessore, Khulna, Barisal. This region has two divisions. **Jessore Area.** 55 Infantry Division. 9th Bengal Lancers Regiment, 55th Artillery Brigade, 3rd East Bengal Regiment, 21st Infantry Brigade, 88th Infantry Brigade, 105th Infantry Brigade, Jessore. **Barisal Area.** 7 Infantry Division, Lebukhali, 26th Horse Regiment, Lebukhali; 7th Artillery Brigade, Lebukhali; 6th Infantry Brigade, Lebukhali; 26th Infantry Brigade, Lebukhali

Northern Bangladesh or area north of Padma River and West of Meghna River. This area has borders with Bihar, North Bengal and Western Assam. The main towns in this region are Rajshahi, Bogra, Dinajpur, Rangpur, Thakurgaon. This area has two divisions. **Bogra Area.** 11 Infantry Division. 93rd Armoured Brigade, 5th East Bengal Regiment, 26 Infantry Brigade, 11 Infantry Brigade. 11 Artillery Brigade is located at Jahangirabad. **Rangpur Area.** 66 Infantry Division. 7th Horse Regiment, Rangpur, 66th Artillery Brigade, Kholahati. 34th Bangladesh Infantry Regiment, Rangpur, 72nd Infantry Brigade, Rangpur. 222nd Infantry Brigade, Saidpur. 16th Infantry Brigade, Kholahati.

Eastern Bangladesh or area east of Meghna River. This region has borders with Meghalaya, Tripura, Manipur and Myanmar. The main towns in this region are Mymensingh, Sylhet, Comilla, and Chittagong. This region has five divisions, two facing India, two facing Myanmar and one in depth. **Chittagong Area.** 24 Infantry Division. 15 Bengal Cavalry Regiment, 18 Bangladesh Infantry Regiment, 24 Artillery Brigade at Guimara, 69th Infantry Brigade, Bandarban, 203rd Infantry Brigade, Khagrachhari, 305th Infantry Brigade, Rangamati, 65th Infantry Brigade, Kaptai, ADHOC Artillery Brigade, Kaptai. **Comilla Area.** 33 Infantry Division. 6th Bengal Cavalry Regiment, 33rd Artillery Brigade, 17th Bangladesh Infantry Regiment, 44th Infantry Brigade, 101st Infantry Brigade, Comilla. **Ghatail Area.** 19 Infantry Division, 4th Horse Regiment, 19th Artillery Brigade, 25th Bangladesh Infantry R,egiment, 309 Infantry Brigade, all at Ghatail; 77th Infantry Brigade, Mymensingh and 98 Infantry Brigade, Bhuapur. **Sylhet Area.** 17 Infantry Division, Jalalabad; 17th Artillery Brigade, Jalalabad; 40th Bangladesh Infantry Regiment, Sylhet; 11th Infantry Brigade, Sylhet; 52nd Infantry Brigade, Jalalabad; 360th Infantry Brigade, Jalalabad. **Cox's Bazar Area.** 10 Infantry Division, Ramu; 16th Bengal Cavalry Regiment, Ramu; 10th Artillery Brigade, Ramu; 36th Bangladesh Infantry Regiment, Ramu; 2nd Infantry Brigade, Ramu; 97th Infantry Brigade, Alikadam·

Analysis

Pakistan had only three divisions to protect East Pakistan. This was increased to four during 1971 War. The need for an economically weak country like Bangladesh to have ten divisions is difficult to explain. General Ershad, who was anti-India, had raised the strength of the Bangladesh Army to seven Divisions. Now that strength has risen to ten. The Indian Army Chief recently down-played Bangladesh's growing military capability by saying Bangladesh is a friendly country. **Is it wise to ignore Bangladesh's** significant military might? If aligned with China, it could play a very significant role in severing North-East from mainland India at the Siliguri Corridor.

India

Indian Army

(Source: en.wikipedia.org/wiki/Indian_Army_Organization, adda237.com/defence-jobs/structure of the Indian Army, dehradundefenceacademy.com>indian-army-command-centres-location). This section should be studied with a Google Map of India on a laptop by those who understand military strategy and tactics.

The Indian Army has 40 divisions in 14 corps, 6 Commands and one training command. It has 65 armoured regiments, 50 mechanized infantry Battalions including 10 recce and support battalions. Location of Indian Army Formations are listed below.

Eastern Command: Its headquarter is in Kolkata. it has twelve divisions and four Corps. The locations are III Corps at Dimapur, IV Corps at Tezpur and XXXIII Corps, headquartered at Siliguri, XVII Corps at Panagarh. 23rd Infantry Division – Ranchi, 2nd Mountain Division – Dibrugarh, 5tare listedh Mountain Division – Bomdila, 17th Mountain Division – Gangtok, 56th Mountain Division – Zakhama, 21st Mountain Division – Rangia, 20th Mountain Division – Binnaguri, 57th Mountain Division – Leimakhong, 71st Mountain Division – Missamari, 27th Mountain Division – Kalimpong, 59th Infantry Division –Panagarh and 72 Infantry Division – Pathankot (this division is located outside Eastern Command).

Central Command: Its headquarter situated in Lucknow. As of now, it has no fighting formations under command. Its I Corps is currently assigned to South Western Command.

Northern Command: Its headquarter is in Udhampur. Currently it has three corps, seven divisions, one brigade. XIV Corps – Leh, XV Corps – Srinagar, XVI Corps – Nagrota, 3rd Infantry Division – Leh, 19th Infantry Division – Baramulla, 10th Infantry Division – Akhnoor, 8th Mountain Division – Dras, 28th Mountain Division – Gurez, 25th Infantry Division – Rajauri, 39th Infantry Division – Yol, 10 Artillery brigade

Southern Command: Its headquarter is situated in Pune. At present it has two corps, six divisions and three brigades. XII Corps – Jodhpur, XXI Corps – Bhopal, 41st Artillery Division – Pune, 11th Infantry Division – Ahmedabad, 31st Armoured Division – Jhansi, 12th RAPID– Jodhpur, 36th RAPID – Sagar, 54th Infantry Division – Secundrabad, 4th Armoured

Brigade, 340th Mechanised Brigade, 475th Engineering Brigade

South-Western Command: This command has its headquarters in Jaipur. Currently two corps, seven divisions and three brigades. I Corps – Mathura, X Corps – Bhatinda. 42nd Artillery Division – Jaipur, 4th Infantry Division – Allahabad, 16th Infantry Division – Sri Ganganagar, 6th Mountain Division – Bareilly, 18th RAPID – Kota, 33rd Armoured Division – Hisar, 24th RAPID – Bikaner, 6th Independent Armoured Brigade, 615th Independent Air Defence Brigade and 471st Engineering Brigade.

Western Command: Its headquarter is situated in Chandigarh. At present this command has three corps, nine divisions, three independent armoured brigades, one mechanized infantry brigade, one air defence brigade and one engineer brigade. II Corps – Ambala, IX Corps – Yol – Dharamsala (Himachal Pradesh), XI Corps – Jalandhar. 40th Artillery Division – Ambala, 1st Armoured Division – Patiala, 26th Infantry Division – Jammu, 7th Infantry Division – Firozpur, 14th RAPID – Dehradun, 29th Infantry Division – Pathankot, 9th Infantry Division – Meerut, 22nd Infantry Division – Meerut, 15th Infantry Division – Amritsar, 2nd Independent Armoured Brigade, 3rd Independent Armoured Brigade, 23rd Armoured Brigade, 612th Mechanised Independent Air Defence Brigade, 474th Engineering Brigade, 55th Mechanised Brigade.

India's Air Defence Capability

The Indian Ballistic Missile Defence Program is designed to counter the ballistic missile threat from Pakistan and China. It is a two-tiered system consisting of two land and sea-based interceptor missiles, including the Prithvi Air Defence (PAD) missile for High Altitude interception, and the Advanced Air Defence (AAD) Missile for lower altitude interception. The two-tiered shield is meant to intercept a ny incoming missile launched from 5,000 kilometres away. The system also includes an overlapping network of early warning and tracking radars, as well as command and control posts. As per reports emerged in January 2020, the first phase of BMD program is now complete. The Indian Air Force and DRDO are in charge of the program. The status of the program is not in public domain. (**Source: en.wikipedia.org/wiki/Indian_Ballestic_Missile_Defence_ Programe**).

Indian Missile Program

(**Source:** en.wikipedia.org/wiki/ Intigrated_Guided_Missile_Development_Program ; en.wikipedia. org/ List_of_India_Military_Missiles)

Dr. APJ Abdul Kalam had started development of Indian Guided Missiles. It is one of the most successful wings of DRDO.

Surface to Air Missiles. Surface to air missile Trishul has been in service since 1983. **Akash MKI** is a medium-range surface-to-air missile has been accepted by Indian Air Force 2009. The Indian Air Force has placed orders for eight squadrons of the Akash system. QRSAM, A quick reaction SAM and VL-MRSAM were inducted in 2022. Barak 8 MRSAM and LRSAM were inducted into service in 2020 and 2020 respectively. Russian S 400 is in service since 2021.

Anti-tank Missile Nag is a third generation, all-weather, anti-tank missile. Separate versions for the Army and the Air Force are being developed. Nag Prospina and its heli-borne version HeliNa were introduced into service in 2016.

Surface to Surface Ballistic missiles These are in different categories; Short Range Ballistic Missiles (SRBM), Medium Range Ballistic Missile (MRBM), Submarine Launched Ballistic Missiles (SLBM). **SRBM** Prithvi is in service. SRBMs Prahar, range 150km; Pragati, range 170km; Pranash, range 200km are being developed. Pralay, a short-range surface to surface ballistic missile is also under development. **MRBMs** Agni -I, Agni-P, Agni-III, Agni-IV, Agni-V with ranges from 1200km to 8000km have been inducted into service between 2002 to 2018. Agni-VI with a range of 16,000 km is being developed. All these missiles can carry nuclear warheads. **Submarine launched SLBM**, K 15 Sagarika has been introduced into service in 2018. A submarine launched BrahMos is also in service since 2018.

Surface to surface anti-ship missile, Dhanush has been introduced into service in 2018. BrahMos A anti-ship missile is in service since 2019.

In **cruise missiles** India has BrahMos I, II and III in service. Nirbhaya LAM was introduced into service in 2019.

Air to Air Missiles. Astra MKI air to air missile is in service since 2019. Novator KS 172 has been in service since 2009.

Many more missiles are in various stages of development. India thus has a large range of various types of missiles. However, whether they are available in the required numbers is a question or military leaders must examine.

Artillery

The Field Artillery Rationalization Plan of 2010 of the army plans to procure 3000 to 4000 units of artillery at the cost of ₹200 billion (US$2 billion). This includes purchasing 1580 towed, 814 mounted, 180 self-propelled wheeled, 100 self-propelled tracked, and 145 ultra-light 155 mm/ 39 calibre guns. The FARP was further amplified by the Artillery Profile 2027, which was drafted in year 2008. In 2023, the CAG reported that only 8% of the had been received. The requirement for artillery guns would be met with indigenous development and production. The Army has ordered 114 Dhanush Howitzers. The Advanced Towed Artillery Gun System (ATAGS) developed by DRDO in collaboration with production partners, Bharat Forge and Tata Advanced Systems forms a part of Indian Army's artillery modernisation plan. In May 2022, the ATAGS successfully completed trials. 20 March 2025, the procurement of 307 ATAGS and 327 gun-towing vehicles to arm 15 artillery regiments at an estimated cost of around ₹7,000 crore has been approved. The Army also has plans to procure 1,200 155mm Towed Gun Systems (TGS). The initial order for 400 units was granted on 30 November 2023. The trials of contenders of TGS tenders are set to commence in 2025. The Indian Army plans to procure 200 units of 105mm L/37 mounted howitzers. The project is at prototype stage. It also plans to procure 814 units of 155mm L/52 calibre Mounted Guns. The guns should have a maximum range of more than 38 km, have a maximum weight of 30 tonnes and should be able to fire all existing 155 mm rounds in the Indian Army's inventory. The gun is under development. The Indian Army is planning to induct wheeled delf-propelled guns between 2025 and 2027. In 2017, the Government of India approved purchase 100 K9 Vajra-T tracked self-propelled guns. India has procured 145 M777 155mm L/39 ultra-light howitzer from USA. (**Source: en.wikipedia.org/wiki/Field_Artillery_Rationalization_Plan)**

In multiple rocket launchers, we have the Pinaka MKI in service. Many variations of Pinaka with better ranges is under development.

It will be seen that there has been no physical addition to Indian Army's field artillery capability except for the 145 ultra-light howitzers.

India Airforce

India's Drone Capability

Source: baalnoiacademy.com/drones_in_Indian_armed_forces, **en.wikipedia.org/wiki/Category: unmanned_miltary_aircraft_of_India)**

UAVs or drones as popularly called nnare an essential tool of modern warfare. They are low-cost, low-risk, high payoff intelligence, surveillance and reconnaissance (ISR) and target acquisition (TA) systems.

Nishant. This drone has been developed by DRDO. It is for intelligence gathering over enemy territory and for reconnaissance, training, surveillance, target designation, artillery fire correction, damage assessment. The UAV requires rail-launching from a hydro-pneumatic launcher and recovered by a parachute system.

Heron. It is a reconnaissance and surveillance drone. India had about 12 Heron-1 drones in 2004. The Heron UAV is reportedly capable of flying for over 24 hours at a time at altitudes around 32,000 feet. TIt is a large Medium Altitude, Long Endurance UAV, built to carry multiple payloads at a time for a variety of missions. The Indian government had approved the purchase of ten **Heron TP** drones of Israeli designs. These will be operated by the Indian Air Force, with Harpy loitering munitions.

Harpy. The Harpy is a loitering munition produced by Israel Aerospace Industries. The Harpy is designed to attack radar systems and is optimised for the SEAD role. It carries a high explosive warhead. It has a maximum speed of 185 km/hr and 500 km range of flight. India has purchased it.

Searcher. The Indian Army has reportedly deployed its first batch of 25 Israeli-made Searcher Mark II unmanned aerial vehicles (UAVs) over its frontiers with Pakistan and China. India had purchased 100 of the reconnaissance drones. The Indian Army operates both Searcher Mk I and II. The Searcher Mark II is produced by Israel Aircraft Industries. It can remain airborne for 16 hours and has a maximum range of 150 km at the relatively high altitude of 18,500 feet, making it especially suitable for missions over the Himalayas.

Rustom. This is a target acquisition and reconnaissance drone. It has three variants, Rustom-I, Rustom-H, Rustom-II. It is manufactured by HAL for use by Army, Navy and Airforce.

Netra. The Netra is an Indian, light-weight drone for surveillance and reconnaissance operations. Netra is launched from a small clearing, and it can fly up to a distance of 2.5 km from its take-off point. It can carry out surveillance in an area of 1.5 km Line of Sight (LOS) at the height of 300 m, for 30 minutes on a single battery charge. It has a high-resolution camera with zoom to facilitate more comprehensive surveillance and can also carry a thermal camera for night operations.

Predator Guardian Drones from US. The US has cleared the sale of predator Guardian drones to India. India is looking to buy 22 predator Guardian drones from the US for $2 billion.

Analysis

India has been using drones for intelligence, surveillance, and reconnaissance sorties along the Line of Actual Control (LAC), over the

Bay of Bengal, Andaman and Nicobar Islands and Arabian Sea, and areas around Maldivian waters. Indian Armed Forces do not have armed drone capability. To date, the Indian military only operates drones from Israel for surveillance and reconnaissance missions.

China, Pakistan, and perhaps even Bangladesh is ahead of India in use of drones as a weapon system. Kamikaze attack drones are being used in Ukraine and Israel making the use of fighter aircraft almost unnecessary. India must develop and produce armed drones.

India's Defence Production Capability

India has till recently been the world's largest purchaser of defence equipment. Recently, it has been overtaken by Ukraine. India lags far behind China in production of military hardware. Even Iran and North Korea produce more military hardware than India does.

Comparison of Troops in Areas of Interest

Border With Pakistan. Pakistan is the only country on our western borders. Pakistan Army has a total of eight corps consisting of two armoured divisions, four mechanized divisions, fifteen infantry divisions and two artillery division. one Special Security Division, one division-sized formation called Northern Areas Command (operates in POK), one engineer division. and three artillery divisions. These are distributed five military regions, Punjab, Sindh, J&K FANA, NWFP & FATA and Baluchistan. **Punjab** has two armoured divisions, one mechanized division, five infantry divisions, one artillery division, and one engineer division. **Sindh Military Region** has one mechanized division and two infantry divisions.**J&K and FANA Military Region** has Northern Area Command (POK) and three infantry divisions. **NWFP / FATA Military Region and Baluchistan Military Region** has two infantry divisions each but **they are not on the Indian border.**

Thus, the total troops Pakistan has facing India are two armoured divisions, four mechanized divisions, eleven infantry divisions, three artillery divisions. Northern area command (o ne division) and one engineer division.

Indian Troops on Western Borders

India has three commands and XV Corps of Northern Command facing Pakistan. Southern Command has one armoured division, two Rapid Divisions, two infantry divisions, one artillery division, one independent armoured brigade, one mechanized infantry brigade and one engineer brigade. South Western Command has one armoured division, two Rapid divisions, two infantry divisions, one mountain division, one artillery division, one independent armoured brigade, one air defence brigade and one engineer brigade. Western Command has one armoured division, one artillery division, One RAPID Division, six infantry divisions, three independent armoured brigades, one mechanized brigade, one mechanized air defence brigade, and one Engineer Brigade. Northern Command has four infantry divisions, one mountain division and one artillery brigade.

Thus, India has three armoured divisions, five RAPID divisions, fourteen infantry divisions, two mountain divisions, two artillery divisions, five independent armoured brigades, two mechanized infantry brigades, two air defence brigades, one independent artillery brigade, and two engineer brigades.

Analysis

BothIndia andPakistan are nuclear powers and all-out war between the two is extremely unlikely. Both armies are equally matched in Punjab and Jammu and Kashmir. Against Pakistan's twelve infantry divisions, India has fourteen infantry divisions and two mountain divisions. India has one armoured division and three independent armoured brigades more than Pakistan. In my opinion, India can transfer two infantry divisions and one armoured brigade along with a corps headquarters to protect the Siliguri Corridor without compromising its defences against Pakistan.

Comparison of troops on LAC with China.

The entire LAC is directly under the Central Military Commission and divided into Xinjiang Military District which is responsible for the Ngari District of Tibet and Tibet Military District which is responsible for the rest of the LAC. This should be seen in two stretched; Daulat Beg Oldie in Ladak to China/Nepal/India tri junction in Uttarakhand **(Western LAC)** and Sikkim, North Bengal and Arunachal **(Eastern LAC).**

Western LAC. China. Xinjiang Military District

The Xinjiang Military District is directly under the Central Military Commission. It a is responsible for Xinjiang and Ngari District of Tibet. It is in charge of the disputed area of Aksai Chin and the LAC in Ladakh. It has four combined arms division of which **two appear to be for Ladakh.** It has fifteen **Border Defence regiments of which four are on the LAC.** In addition it has 84 Special Forces Brigade, Kasgarh; 84 Army Aviation Brigade, Changi; 84 Artillery Brigade, Urumqi, 84 Air Defence Brigade, Urumqi; 6 intelligence and Surveillance Brigade, Urumqi; 6 Information Support Brigade, Urumqi; 6 Electronic Countermeasure Brigade, Urumqi;

4 motorized Transport Brigade, 3 Motorized Transport Regiment, 1st Communication Regiment, 2nd Communication Regiment, 2nd Chemical Defence Regiment, 9th Combat Engineer Regiment and Construction Engineer Regiment, Rutog, Ngari Prefecture. Of the fifteen border defence regiments, two are located in Ngari Prefecture; 361 Border Defence Regiment, Tsamda County and 362 Border Defence Regiment, Rutog. 363 Border Defence Regiment Located at Sahidulla, Pishan County, Hotan Prefecture and the 362 Border Defence Regiment were engaged in the fighting with India Army at Galwan and Pangan Tso in 2020.

76th Group Army, HQ Xining, Qinghai. it consists of six CABs (equivalent of two divisions), In addition it has 76th Special Operations Brigade, 76th Army Aviation Brigade, 76th Artillery Brigade, 76th Air Defence Brigade, 76th Engineering and Chemical Defence Brigade and 76th Service Support Brigade.

Thus, China has a total of four divisions and four Border Guards Regiments along with artillery and other supporting arms on the Western LAC.

Western LAC. India. India's Northern Command is responsible for the Western LAC. It has one corps, XIV, two divisions, 3 Mountain Division at Leh and 8 Mountain Division at Gurez, units of Ladakh Scouts and other para-militaries and supporting arms.

Analysis. It will be seen that the Chinese troops of Xinjiang Military District and XIV Corps of India are evenly matched in troops if not in supporting arms. If China uses 76th Group Army for attack, India will have to reinforce XIV Corps with its strategic reserves.

Eastern LAC China

The Eastern LAC can be divided into two. The LAC between Nepal and Bhutan and the LAC in Arunachal Pradesh. Sikkim and West Bengal has borders with Tibet in this Sector. The Yadong and ... Prefectures are on the other side. Tibet Military District is in charge of the entire LAC. The entire LAC comes under Western Theatre Command of China. On the Indian side XXXIII Corps is responsible for LAC between Nepal and Bhutan. IV Corps and III Corps are responsible the LAC in Arunachal. Overall responsibility for the Eastern LAC on Indian side is Eastern Command.

Tibet Military District

The Military District is under the Army HQ and only administratively under Western Theatre Command. It is commanded by a Lt. Gen. and its HQ is located at Lhasa. It has three combined arms brigade, one special operations brigade, one Army Aviation Brigade; one Artillery Brigade; one Air-Defence Brigade; one Engineering and Chemical Brigade; one Electronic Countermeasures Brigade; one Motorized Transport Brigade and Tibet Military Region Communication Regiment. The Tibet Military District has thirteen to fourteen Border Guard Regiments; 351st Border Guard Regiment, Zayu County, Nyingchi prefecture; 352nd Border Guard Regiment, Medog County, Nyingchi Prefecture; 353rd Border Guard Regiment, Mainling City, Nyingchi Prefecture; 354th Border Guard Regiment, Lhunze County, Lhoka Prefecture; 355th Border Guard Regiment, Cona County, Lhoka Prefecture; 356th Border Guard Regiment, Yadong County, Shigatse Prefecture: 357th Border Guard Regiment, Tingri County, Shigaste Prefecture and 358th Border Guard Regiment, Saga County, Shigatse Prefecture; 1 Border Guard Regiment, Shannan City, Longzi County, 2 Border Guard Regiment, Cuona County; 3rd Border Guards Regiment, Shigaste, Tingri County; 4th Border Regiment, Chyau, Linzhi County; 5th Border Regiment, Saga County; 6th Border Regiment, Yadong County, .

77th Group Army. Chongzhou, Chengdu, Sichwan. It consists of six CABs, In addition it has 77th Special Operations Brigade, 77th Army Aviation Brigade – Operates MI-17 helicopters; 77th Artillery Brigade; 77th Air Defence Brigade, 77th Engineering Brigade, 77th Chemical Defence Brigade and 7reorganization of the Chinese 7th Service Support Brigade.

Other units under Western Theatre Command are Third Brigade of Reconnaissance Intelligence, third Brigade of Information Support, third Brigade of Electronic Warfare, 53 Mountain Motorized Infantry Brigade and 54th Brigade.

Thus, China has the equivalent of two divisions and fourteen Border Guards Regiments on the Eastern LAC. 77th Group Army with about two division and additional supporting arms are available for offensives.

Eastern LAC. India.

The Eastern LAC can be divided into two. The LAC between Nepal and Bhutan and the LAC in Arunachal Pradesh. Sikkim and West Bengal has borders with Tibet in this Sector. On the Indian side XXXIII Corps having three divisions is responsible for LAC between Nepal and Bhutan. IV Corps and III Corps are responsible the LAC in Arunachal. IV Corps has four divisions, III Corps has 3 of which two could deploy on LAC. Overall responsibility for the Eastern LAC on Indian side is Eastern Command. Its headquarter is in Kolkata. it has XVII Corps at Panagarh as reserve. This

Corps has three divisions. 23rd Infantry Division – Ranchi, 59th Infantry Division –Panagarh and 72 Infantry Division – Pathankot (this division is located outside Eastern Command).

Analysis. It will be seen that the Chinese troops of Tibet Military District are less than XXIII Corps and IV Corps of India in troops if not in supporting arms. If China uses 77th Group Army for attack, India will have adequate forces in XXXIII and IV Corps to defend the LAC.

Analysis

India has adequate troops to defend the LAC against a Chinese attack. However, it is inferior in artillery, drones, missiles, and air power. China has better communications from their bases to the borders and infrastructure for housing troops at the border in the form of dual-purpose villages.

Bangladesh

India's border with Bangladesh will be examined in three sections; border with Western Bangladesh extending from Farraka to the Sundarbans, Northern Bangladesh extending from Farraka to Brahmaputra/ Meghna River and Meghna River to Burma Border.

Bangladesh has ten divisions. **Western Bangladesh** has two divisions 55 Infantry Division at Jessore and 7 Infantry Division at Barisal. India also has two divisions in this sector, 59 Infantry Divisionat Panagarh and 23 Infantry Division at Ranchi. **Northern Bangladesh** has two divisions, 11 Infantry Division at Bogra and 66 Infantry Division at Rangpur. This area is with XXXIII Corps of India. This Corps has three divisions. They are mostly oriented to defend the LAC. **Eastern Bangladesh** has five divisions, two facing India, two facing Myanmar and one in depth. 33 Infantry Division is at Comilla opposite Tripura19 Infantry Division is at Ghatail in depth,17 Infantry Division is at Jalalabad. Indian III Corps is perhaps responsible for this border. It has one division at Leimakong and one division at Zakhama.

Analysis

Bangladesh has possibly never been seen as a threat. Whereas India and Bangladesh have parity of divisions in Western Bangladesh and Eastern Bangladesh, India has nothing much opposite Northern Bangladesh which is opposite the sensitive **Siliguri Corridor**. It should also be noted that each Bangladesh division has an armoured regiment and there is an armoured brigade at Dhaka. That gives Bangladesh thirteen armoured regiments. I am not sure that Eastern Command has adequate armour to match Bangladesh in mechanised forces.

Some other Aspects of Warfare.

Numerical Strength is not Decisive. Numerical strength of armies does not reflect their fighting capability. For example, in a Indian infantry division of about 12,000, the infantry element is only three brigades. Each brigade has three battalions. Each battalion has four rifle companies of about 120 soldiers. During war, only about 90 to 100 men are expected to be available. **Thus, an infantry division can produce only about 3600 infantry soldiers.** The rest of the numbers go to man headquarters, artillery, other weapon system, engineers, signals, drivers, langar staff, administrative units, medical personnel, cooks, mess staff etc.

Training, morale and fighting spirit is more important than numbers. During the 1947-48 Kashmir war, one company of Kashmir State forces of about a hundred men defended the Skardu Fort for more than 100 days against the Pakistan Army. These brave forgotten soldiers fought to the last man, till ammunition and food ran out. In the process they gave time to the Indian Army to deploy forces at Kargil and Ladakh and prevented these areas falling into Pakistani hands. In contrast, in 1962, one mountain division, deployed in prepared defences with large stocks of ammunition and rations at Sela fled in face of the Chinese attack without a fight and opened the road to Guwahati to the Chinese without a fight. Two divisions of Iraqi army tasked to defend Mosul left their weapons and fled in the face of 400 ISIS militants approaching in small trucks. Four divisions of the Afghan Army surrendered to the Taliban without a fight when the US troops left. Hamas has not surrendered to the Israeli army.

It is sad that our political and military leaders do not care about the morale and fighting spirit of our soldiers. **Affiliation to their regiment, good junior leadership and jawan-officer comraderies, adequate leave, rest, and time with families are essential for good morale and will to fight.** None of the conditions are met today. There is a large shortage of troops. Agniveer recruitment will finish regimental spirit. Jawans are retiring but recruitment has stopped. There is an acute shortage of jawans and junior officers and there is hardly any bonding between officers and men. No one gets full leave. Number of suicides are large. Who cares?

Quality of Generals Matter. Generals win battles. Alexander the Great, Hanibal, Napolean, Rommel, O'Conner, Patton, McArthur are generals who routinely defeated larger armies. Babar defeated a larger army of Ibrahim Lodi. Ahmad Shah Abdali defeated the massive Maratha Army at the Third Battle of Panipat. Brig. L P Sen successfully defended Srinagar against much larger Pakistani force at the Battle of Shalteng ("Grandpa's Selection:

Outstanding Victories of the Indian Army" by Col Retd Bhaskar Sarkar VSM, Notion Press.com. available on Amazon and Flipkart). Conversely, Lt Gen BM Kaul, commanding 4 Corps in 1962, reported sick and fled to Delhi from Tezpur. His operation plan of holding defences based on the Namka Chu (basing defences on a fordable stream in the mountains instead of basing them on defensible ridge lines was a primary reason for the defeat.) General Thapar, who became army chief super-ceding General J N Chowdhury due to his pliable nature, who had approved general Kaul's operational plans, had to be sacked after the 1962 debacle. It is not out of place to mention that General J N Choudhury was elevated to be the Army Chief after the Chinese debacle and helped to revive the Indian Army and enabled it to hold Pakistan in 1965. General Sagat Singh's bold leadership and strategic planning enabled his 4 Corps to reach Dhaka in just 17 days during the 1971 War. He routed two Pakistani divisions on the way.

Do we have competent generals leading the Army? We, the people of India, will know if we are tested.

Logistic Planning. Logistic during war, stocking of ammunition, POL, bridging material, rations, resupply of these items to the fighting forces, evacuation and treatment of casualties need careful planning. Inadequate attention to this aspect can result in disaster. That is what happened in the initial days of the Ukraine War. Russian armoured forces advanced from the Belarus Border on 24 February 2022 and reached almost up to Kiev. The 85 km long armoured column remained on the road till April 2022. Then, running out of fuel, ammunition and food, the leading Russian troops surrendered. Those at the rear withdrew into Russia and saved themselves. A war that was almost over in one month with almost no casualties is still going on after 3 years. Hundreds of thousands have died on both sides. (en.wikipedia.org/wiki/Russian_Invasion_of_Ukraine).

Mrs. Indira Gandhi wanted the Indian Army to launch operations to liberate East Pakistan in April 1971. General Manekshaw, the Army Chief told her that the Army was not ready and explained to her the logistic preparations that were necessary. Mrs. Gandhi relented. Preparations started in full swing. By December 1971, preparations were completed. Rest is history. India's liberation of East Pakistan and creation of Bangladesh has no parallel in post-World War II history.

Do we have a logistic plan to defend India in a long war with China supported by Pakistan and Bangla Desh? Our political and military leaders must be aware of the logistic preparedness. We the people of India will know if we are attacked.

Passive Defensive Measuring. The Wars in Ukraine and between Israel and Hamas and Hezbollah has amply demonstrated the destructive power of fighters, bombers, missiles, and drones. Russian cities up to 800 km from Ukraine border are being daily attacked with missiles and drones and suffering heavy damage to oil refineries, air fields and industrial infrastructure. Russians, with their air defence systems including S-400 are only able to destroy about 80% to 90% of the missiles and drones.

Israil air strikes have reduced Gaza to rubble and caused considerable damage to Beirut and other areas of Lebanon. Hamas and Hezbollah do not have any viable air defence. Yet they have not been defeated after 15 months of daily strikes. This is because they have constructed Kms and kms of tunnels deep underground for shelters for men, ammunition, weapon systems and rations. Iran has done the same. Israel has all its fighter air craft in underground hangers. Tunnels have been used by North Vietnam to safeguard its people and military hardware during the Korean War. Al Qaeda used tunnels at Tora Bora to escape US air strikes and drone strikes.

It is not cost effective for a large country like India to acquire active air defence (anti-aircraft missile systems, anti-missile missile systems and anti-drone weapon systems). Passive air defence systems like tunnels and under-ground shelters is the only way we can protect our troops, warlike stores, ammunition, weapon systems, aircraft and logistic infrastructure. India has the technological capability to dig long and wide tunnels.

Do our armed forces have any plan for building tunnels and underground shelters for passive defence against Chinese and Pakistani air strikes, missiles and drones? Our political and military leaders must be aware of the state of preparedness. We, the people of India will only know if and when we are attacked.

Duration of War. India has seen only short wars. The longest, Kashmir War 1947-48 lasted from 22 Oct 1947 to 5 Jan 1948 or about 75 days. The 1965 War lasted a little over a month from Aug 1965 to 22 Sep 1965. The 1971 War lasted just 13 days from 3Dec 1971 to 16 Dec 1971. The 1999 Kargil War lasted from 3 May to 26 Jul 1999. However, this was a localized war with only one Indian division being involved in evicting the enemy and recapturing Indian territories.

But there is no guarantee that future wars if any with China, Pakistan and Bangla Desh will be as short. Iraq-Iran War lasted 8 years. Russia- Ukraine War has been going on for almost 3 years. Israel-Hamas-Hezbollah war has been going on for one year and a half.

Are our armed forces prepared for a long war? Do we have enough stocks of ammunition and weapon systems to fight a long war? Do we have any contingency plan for fighting a long war? Pur political and military leaders must be well aware of our capabilities and plans. We the people of India will only know when we are tested.

National Priorities are Decisive in Defence Preparedness. National Priorities determine defence preparedness. From 1947 to 1962, Congress Government under Pandit Nehru relegated defence preparedness to unnecessary. He diverted all available funds towards development of the country. After the Chinese Debacle of 1962, things changed. Lal Bahadur Shastri and after him Mrs. Indira Gandhi modernized the Indian Army and liberated Bangla Desh in 1971. The Indian Army was at its peak defence preparedness during the time of Rajeev Gandhi. He sent an airborne force into Sri Lanka to protect Sri Lankan Tamils and later fought an inconclusive war against the LTTE. The slump started when Shri Narsimha Rao was the Prime Minister. His deal with IMF restricted defence expenditure to less than 3% of GDP. Stagnation for promotion amongst senior army officers gave rise to "Yes-manship"; "No mistake syndrome" and other unethical practices. Intake of officers was reduced to address the promotion stagnation to the detriment of operational readiness and officer-jawan camaraderie. Things did not change during Manmohan Singh's time as Prime Minister. Cosmetic improvements like creating the post of Chief of Defence Staff (CDS), theatre commands and import of some high-profile items have taken place under the present government. But the question still remains in some of us; **"Are we prepared for a long war with China and its allies Pakistan and Bangla Desh?"**

India has always been one of the world's largest importers of military hardware. China has strived to enhance its indigenous capability to produce its requirement of military hardware. It initially relied on Soviet technology but over the years developed its defence related industries. It even produces stealth fighters and all types of missiles and drones. Today, China not only produces its own requirement of all kinds of military hardware but also sell weapon systems to all its allies like Pakistan, Bangla Desh, Myanmar, Nepal etc.

India also had opportunities to produce indigenous weapon systems. It was producing Gnat fighters in 1971 but stopped. It produced MIG engines for MIG 21 but did not upgrade or diversify its capabilities to indigenously produce engines for its military aircrafts. Not that it cannot. If India can produce engines for rockets for satellite and space program, why should it not be capable of producing engines for its fighter aircraft and helicopters?

There are three reasons. The first is Qualitative Requirements (QR) spelled out by the military brass for development by DRDO. The method adopted is to take out the book "Jane's Weapon Systems," view the capabilities of the selected equipment, select the best available capability, and put it in the QR. It is impossible to meet such a QR. If, while looking for a bride for my son I put the QR as beautiful as Aishwariya Rai Bachchan, as intelligent as Shakuntala Devi, as wealthy as Nita Ambani and a singer like Lata Mangeshkar, you can be sure that my son will remain unmarried. A QR has to be achievable. All countries which produce weapon systems started with workable models and kept improving the capabilities. If we want to become a weapon system producer, we must start the assembly line with whatever the DRDO and its industry partner can produce and keep improving the models.

The second reason is kick-backs. Defence deals with foreign countries always come with kick-backs which our politicians cannot resist.

The third reason is the allocation of funds. As we have seen, the DRDO budget is about Rs 7000 crores. The allocation for animal husbandry and dairy development is Rs 29,110 crores for three years (www.dadh.gov.in). It will be clear where the priority lies.

Summary

Comparison of Armed Forces of Pakistan, China, Bangladesh and India

Chinese Armed Forces. The New Border Law which came into force on January 1, 2022 prevents China from giving up any territory that historically was a part of it. So military and diplomatic negotiations between India and China are meaningless. India should either be ready to surrender disputed territories including Arunachal Pradesh or get ready to fight.

The Chinese Armed forces are the largest in the world and its air force and navy are the third largest after the US and Russians. With over 2 trillion US dollars as its foreign exchange reserve, it seeks to be the number one military power in the world. It may take fifteen to twenty years to achieve this goal. **But that is not much of a solace to India which is falling behind every year.**

Pakistan Army has a total of eight corps consisting of two armoured divisions, four mechanized divisions, fifteen infantry divisions and two artillery division. one Special Security Division, one division-sized formation called Northern Areas Command (operates in POK), and one engineer division. and three artillery divisions. Four divisions are deployed in Baluchistan and on Afghan border. **India** has three armoured divisions, five RAPID divisions, fourteen infantry divisions, two mountain divisions, two artillery divisions, five independent armoured brigades, two mechanized infantry brigades, two air defence brigades, one independent artillery brigade, and two engineer brigades on. The Pakistan Border. India has a clear superiority in numbers on the Western Front.

Bangladesh has ten divisions. **Western Bangladesh** has two divisions 55 Infantry Division at Jessore and 7 Infantry Division at Barisal. India also has two divisions in this sector, 59 Infantry Divisionat Panagarh and 23 Infantry Division at Ranchi. **Northern Bangladesh** has two divisions, 11 Infantry Division at Bogra and 66 Infantry Division at Rangpur. This area is with XXXIII Corps of India. This Corps has three divisions. They are mostly oriented to defend the LAC. **Eastern Bangladesh** has five divisions, two facing India, two facing Myanmar and one in depth. 33 Infantry Division is at Comilla opposite Tripura19 Infantry Division is at Ghatail in depth,17 Infantry Division is at Jalalabad. Indian III Corps is perhaps responsible for this border. It has one division at Leimakong and one division at Zakhama.

Each Bangladesh Infantry Division has an armoured regiment. In addition, they have two armoured brigades at Bodra and Dhaka. **Thus, Bangladesh has sixteen armoured regiments. Does India's Eastern Command have even one?**

Some other Aspects of Warfare.

Training, morale and fighting spirit is more important than numbers. It is sad that our political and military leaders do not care about the morale and fighting spirit of our soldiers. **Affiliation to their regiment, good junior leadership and jawan-officer comraderies, adequate leave, rest, and time with families are essential for good morale and will to fight.** None of the conditions are met today. Agniveer recruitment will finish regimental spirit. Jawans are retiring but recruitment has stopped. There is an acute shortage of jawans and junior officers and there is hardly any bonding between officers and men. No one gets full leave. Number of suicides are large. Who cares?

Quality of Generals Matter. Brig. L P Sen successfully defended Srinagar against much larger Pakistani force at the Battle of Shalteng (**"Grandpa's Selection: Outstanding Victories of the Indian Army" by Col Retd Bhaskar Sarkar VSM, Notion Press.com. available on Amazon and Flipkart**). Conversely, Lt Gen BM Kaul, commanding 4 Corps in 1962, reported sick and fled to Delhi from Tezpur. General Sagat Singh's bold leadership and strategic planning enabled his IV Corps to reach Dhaka in just 17 days during the 1971 War. He routed two Pakistani divisions on the way. **Do we have competent generals leading the Army?** We, the people of India, will know if we are tested.

Logistic Planning. Logistic during war, stocking of ammunition, POL, bridging material, rations, resupply of these items to the fighting forces, evacuation and treatment of casualties need careful planning. In adequate attention to this aspect can result in disaster. Mrs. Indira Gandhi wanted the Indian Army to launch operations to liberate East Pakistan in April 1971. General Manekshaw, the Army Chief told her that the Army was not ready and explained to her the logistic preparations that were necessary. Mrs. Gandhi relented. India's liberation of East Pakistan and creation of Bangladesh has no parallel in post-World War II history. **Do we have a logistic plan to defend India in a long war with China supported by Pakistan and Bangla Desh?**

Passive Defensive Measures. Wars have never been won by bombing. The US dropped more bombs on Vietnam than total dropped during the World War II and used Napalm, white phosphorus, and Agent Orange. It lost the war. The US bombed Afghanistan for about 13 years. It lost the War. The Wars in Ukraine and between Israel and Hamas and Hezbollah has amply demonstrated the destructive power of fighters, bombers, missiles, and drones. Israil air strikes have reduced Gaza to rubble and caused considerable damage to Beirut and other areas of Lebanon. Hamas and Hezbollah do not have any viable air defence. Yet they have not been defeated after 18 months of daily strikes. This is because they have constructed Kms and kms of tunnels deep underground for shelters for men, ammunition, weapon systems and rations. Iran has done the same. Israel has all its fighter air craft in underground hangers. Tunnels have been used by North Vietnam to safeguard its people and military hardware during the Korean War. Al Qaeda used tunnels at Tora Bora to escape US air strikes and drone strikes.

It is not cost effective for a large country like India to acquire active air defence (anti-aircraft missile systems, anti-missile missile systems and anti-drone weapon systems). Passive air defence systems like tunnels and underground shelters is the only way we can protect our troops, warlike stores, ammunition, weapon systems, aircraft, and logistic infrastructure. India has the technological capability to dig long and wide tunnels. **Do our armed forces have any plan for building tunnels and underground shelters for passive defence against Chinese and Pakistani air strikes, missiles and drones?** Our political and military leaders must be aware of the state of preparedness. We, the people of India will only know if and when we are attacked.

Duration of War. India has seen only short wars. The longest, Kashmir War 1947-48 lasted from 22 Oct 1947 to 5 Jan 1948 or about 75 days. The 1965 War lasted a little over a month from Aug 1965 to 22 Sep 1965. The 1971 War lasted just 13 days from 3Dec 1971 to 16 Dec 1971. The 1999 Kargil War lasted from 3 May to 26 Jul 1999. However, this was a localized war with only one Indian division being involved in evicting the enemy and recapturing Indian territories. But there is no guarantee that future wars if any with China, Pakistan and Bangla Desh will be as short. Iraq-Iran War lasted 8 years. Russia- Ukraine War has been going on for almost 3 years. Israel-Hamas-Hezbollah war has been going on for one year and a half. **Are our armed forces prepared for a long war? Do we have enough stocks of ammunition and weapon systems to fight a long war? Do we have any contingency plan for fighting a long war?**

National Priorities are Decisive in Defence Preparedness. National Priorities determine defence preparedness. From 1947 to 1962, Congress Government under Pandit Nehru relegated defence preparedness to unnecessary. He diverted all available funds towards development of the country. After the Chinese Debacle of 1962, things changed. Lal Bahadur Shastri and after him Mrs. Indira Gandhi modernized the Indian Army and liberated Bangla Desh in 1971. The Indian Army was at its peak defence preparedness during the time of Rajeev Gandhi. He sent an airborne force into Sri Lanka to protect Sri Lankan Tamils and later fought an inconclusive war against the LTTE. The slump started when Shri Narsimha Rao was the Prime Minister. His deal with IMF restricted defence expenditure to less than 3% of GDP. Stagnation for promotion amongst senior army officers gave rise to "Yes-Manship"; "No mistake syndrome" and other unethical practices. Intake of officers was reduced to address the promotion stagnation to the detriment of operational readiness and officer-jawan camaraderie. Things did not change during Manmohan Singh's time as Prime Minister. Cosmetic improvements like creating the post of Chief of Defence Staff (CDS), theatre commands and import of some high-profile items have taken place under the present government. But the question still remains in some of us; **"Are we prepared for a long war with China and its allies Pakistan and Bangla Desh?"**

India has always been one of the world's largest importers of military hardware.

Analysis

India should not be awed by the size of Chinese Armed Forces. What is important is for the Indian military leadership to assess what China can deploy in various sectors of our borders, in what time frame and deploy forces and reserves accordingly. India must deploy adequate early warning and intelligence systems to ensure we are not surprised. Technology and human intelligent must be used. **With the present Chinese focus on Taiwan, it is unlikely that it can deploy any additional troops against India.**

Technological or numerical superiority does not ensure victory in battle. Rome fell to barbarians. Taliban in Afghanistan with no air power or artillery defeated the mighty US and captured enough military equipment to make them a formidable fighting force. Indian armoured units equipped with Second World War vintage Sherman and Centurian tanks defeated Pakistani armoured units equipped with the latest M 47/M 48 American Patton tanks in the battles of Phillora, and Asal Uttar during the 1965 Indo-Pak war. More than a hundred Pakistani tanks were destroyed and 30 new tanks were abandoned on the battle field by the Pakistanis. **The will to fight and will to win, particularly of the infantry and armoured forces, is decisive. China has a three-year contract army comprising of only sons.** Its infantry and armour have not been tested in a hot war since 1979, when they were soundly defeated by Vietnam. **Considering that each Chinese soldier is an only son and a contract soldier, the fighting capability of Chinese infantry and armoured units likely to be poor.**

India needs to adopt offensive defence and dominate the no man's land between troops of the two countries deployed at the LAC. The no use of fire arms is ridiculous. It encourages the Chinese to constantly send patrols into Indian territory knowing that no harm will befall them. They must be discouraged from crossing the LAC.

BothIndia andPakistan are nuclear powers and all-out war between the two is extremely unlikely. Both armies are equally matched in Punjab and Jammu and Kashmir. Against Pakistan's twelve infantry divisions, India has fourteen infantry divisions and two mountain divisions. India has one armoured division and three independent armoured brigades more than Pakistan. **In my opinion, India can transfer two infantry divisions and one armoured brigade along with a corps headquarters to protect the Siliguri Corridor without compromising its defences against Pakistan.**

Bangladesh has possibly never been seen as a threat. Whereas India and Bangladesh have parity of divisions in Western Bangladesh and Eastern Bangladesh, India has nothing much opposite Northern Bangladesh which is opposite the sensitive **Siliguri Corridor.** It should also be noted that each Bangladesh division has an armoured regiment.. That gives Bangladesh ten armoured regiments. They also have two armoured brigades at Bogra and Dhaka. So Bangladesh has sixteen armoured regiments. I am not sure that Eastern Command has adequate armour to match Bangladesh in mechanised forces.

India must immediately makeup the manpower and officer shortages of the Indian Army and scrap Agniveer recruitment for infantry battalions, armoured regiments, and engineer regiments.

India must immediately launch a major drive for passive air defence.

CHAPTER EIGHT

My Threat Perception

I believe that the **Siliguri Corridor is the most vulnerable border area in the whole of India** and it is not adequately defended. In this chapter I am presenting my threat perception for it. Defensive plans are prepared based on several factors such as enemy aims and intentions, terrain, relative strengths, time, and space.

Enemy Aim and Intentions

Pakistan

Let us start with Pakistan. India-Pakistan relations are dominated by two issues; Kashmir and avenging the defeat in 1971. It has attempted to take Kashmir by force four times; 1947-48, 1965, 1971, and 1999. It failed every time. Its economy is weaker than in 1999. Its military equipment is aging. Its army is engaged in insurgency operations in Baluchistan and Pakhtun Khowa region on the Afghan Border. There is political instability. In my mind, the possibility of Pakistan launching another operation to take Kashmir by force is non-existent.

Pakistan would dearly love to see India humiliated by a military defeat and capture of thousands of prisoners. This is mission impossible by itself. However, this aim can be achieved if China and Bangladesh can cutoff India at the Siliguri Corridor. If that happens, China takes Arunachal which it considers its own territory; Assam becomes independent as desired by ULFA whose chief resides in China. The Christian majority tribal states like Nagaland, Mizoram, and hill regions of Manipur, who have ethnic commonality with people across the borders with Myanmar and Bangladesh and are aggrieved by Hindutva push, entry of non-tribals, non-implementation of inner line restrictions, and border fencing will become independent. Meghalaya and Tripura will also become independent. Thousands of troops deployed in these states will be cut off from the Indian mainland and be forced to surrender. Should China attempt to capture

Siliguri Corridor, Pakistan will be delighted to help by launching holding attacks in Kashmir and Rajasthan/Kutch so that Indian troops deployed in these areas cannot be withdrawn to defend the Siliguri Corridor. It could also help Bangladesh with fighter squadrons and other military equipment.

China

China-India relations are strained mainly due to the border dispute and presence of Dalai Lama and Tibetan refugees. China claims that all territories that were historically part of Tibet are Chinese. India on the other hand claims all territories that were a part of British India belong to India. Disputed Aksai Chin is already under Chinese control. The disputed territories in Ladakh and in the central sector are minor. The main area of dispute is Arunachal. China tried to take Arunachal in 1962 and almost did. It withdrew from captured territories in Arunachal either due to logistic difficulties or fear of US intervention. China would like to have Arunachal. Arunachal is presently heavily defended and trying to capture it would be risky.

With Dalai Lama and Tibetan refugees in India, China also apprehends that India at some stage could attempt to liberate Tibet. India is its main rival to dominating Asia and it will be happy to see India cut to size.

Tensions between India and Bangladesh could be seen as an opportunity to cut off India at the Siliguri corridor. Bangladesh could provide much needed military support. It could also solve all the logistic problems that maintaining the troops from mainland China during the winter months would pose. China could deploy some of its air force, missiles and drone assets in Bangladesh.

Bangladesh

India's main problem with Bangladesh is due to the internal politics of that country. Till a third party emerges, there are two main parties, Awami League which in secular and pro-India, and Bangladesh Nationalist Party (BNP) which is Islamist and Pro-Pakistan. Both parties have cordial relations with China which provides Bangladesh with weapon systems and economic aid for infrastructure development. With the ouster of Sheikh Hasina and the Awami League and her presence in India, Bangladesh has moved to the Pakistani camp. This is likely to result in a fillip to military and financial aid to insurgencies in North East India. India's relations with Bangladesh are marred by three issues; India's support for Awami Party and insistence on its being a secular country, India's push to identify and deport Bangladeshis working in India who provide the country with much needed remittances, Indias efforts to stop smuggling of cattle and medicines. The present regime in Bangladesh may also side with China and Pakistan in any major conflict with India.

Terrain

(Refer Map 1 and Google Maps: Yadong Country; Jaldhaka River; Samtse District of Bhutan; Siliguri Corridor and Bangladesh.)

Chumbi Valley, known as **Yadong County** of Shigatze, Tibet lies between Sikkim, India, and Bhutan. Yadong (Yatung), Headquarters of the County, is at the confluence of the Khambu Chu and Tromo Chu rivers, which join to form the Amo Chu River before it flows into India through Bhutan. In India, Amo Chu is named Jaldhaka River. Chinese National Highway connects Yadong to Phari, and Shigatze. It also extends up to the Nathu La pass on the Sikkim border. The south eastern corner, which is actually Bhutanese territory, has been occupied by China. China has built 22 villages in the area. The Doklam Plateau is here.

The point where the borders of India, Tibet China and Bhutan meet is known as the **Zero Point**. There is an Indian Post here. East of Zero Point is the Doklam Plateau. This area is an uninhabited Bhutanese Nature Reserve and is claimed by China. There is a Chinese garrison at Doklam. The Chinese have built a motorable road from Yadong to within a km of Zero Point.

South of Doklam is the Bhutanese Nature Reserve. South of the Nature Reserve is the Samtse District of Bhutan. There is a track/road Samtse-Sipsu Road from Soeltapsa Lhakhang Village in Samtse District of Western Bhutan which runs on the east bank of Jaldhaka River which forms the border between India and Bhutan for some distance. Samtse is the headquarters of the Samtse District of Bhutan. The population of the Samtse district was 60,100 at the 2005 census. Samtse, and Sipsu are close to the Bhutan–India border with roads leading into India. Samtse is connected to Phuntsholing by a highway which runs east-west. A road takes off from near Namlukha Point on this road and heads south towards India passing through Geampakha Monastry to Khanabarti Bridge and on to Gomtu, a border town in south-western Bhutan near the border with India close to Birpara. Gomtu is a small industrial town reachable by road only via India. It is about 70 km west of the large Bhutanese border town of Phuentsholing. This axis can also be used by the Chinese. There are two mountain ranges just north-west and north-east of Samtse which are suitable for defensive positions.

The Jaldhaka Hydel Project is located on the west bank of Jaldhaka River opposite Sipsu in Bhutan. There is a road to the project on the west bank of Jaldhaka River which perhaps goes up to Zero Point. Indian troops located at suitable heights near Jaldhaka Hydel Project will be able to dominate Samtse-Sipsu Road by direct fire.

Analysis

Doklam Plateau and Samtse District of Bhutan (Map 1)

This area is excellent terrain for the Chinese Army to launch an offensive from the Yadong Valley into India. When I was posted at Binaguri in 1965, there used to be an infantry battalion located in a tea garden on the Bhutan Border north of Nagarkata. The Indian border areas are dominated by the hills of Bhutan.

Siliguri Corridor. (Map 2).

I would like to define the Siliguri Corridor as the area of North Bengal that lies between Islampur in the West up to Assam Border in the East and Samtse District of Bhutan to the North and Northern Bangladesh to the South. This area I would like to further subdivide into three sections; area west of Teesta River, area between Teesta and Torsa Rivers and Torsa to Rydak River. Siliguri is a very important transportation node. NH 27 from Purulia to Guwahati Passes through it. Highways to Darjeeling, Kalimpong and Sikkim originate here. There are highways which run west to east through the Siliguri Corridor. NH 27 runs from Siliguri-Jalpaiguri-Mainaguri-Falakata-Alipurduar-Guwahati. NH 17 starts at Sevoke on NH 10 and runs along the Bhutan Border via Chalsa- Banarhat- Hashimara – and joins NH 27 at Alipurduar. There is another road that runs on the canal bank from Siliguri to Teesta Barrage to Lataguri. There are also two railway lines running through the Siliguri Corridor more or less parallel to NH 17 and 27. Bagdogra is the major airport. Cooch Behar also has an airport.

Area West of Teesta River. The area West of Teesta River does not have any border with China or Bhutan. To the North are Darjeeling and Kalimpong districts. To the north west is Nepal. Siliguri, Jalpaiguri, and Bagdogra are the three main towns. NH 27 passes through the area. North of NH 27 is mostly hilly with tea estates interspersed with paddy fields. There is only one river, Mahananda that flows through Siliguri and then veers in south west direction. The Teesta Right Banks canal runs east to west till it flows into Mahananda River. The potential of the canal as an obstacle needs to be evaluated. North Bangladesh lies to the South. The border is not along any obstacle and not very well marked. The terrain is flat with many small rivulets and is suitable for use of armour. There are four main axes in this sector along which Bangladesh can attack; Thakurgaon- Goalpukur - Kishenganj; Thakurgaon -Barakhanti -Islampur; Thkurgaon -Panchagarh -Siliguri; Thakurgaon -Boda- Haldibari -Jalpaiguri.

Area Between Teesta and Torsa Rivers. The area between Teesta River and Torsa River has a common border with Samtse District of Bhutan. There are three routes for Chinese Army to attack India in this sector. The western approach is through Today Tangla Khasmahal – Neora Dam – Gorbathang – Damdim. Next is Zero Point – along west bank of Jaldhaka River – Jaldhaka Hydel Project – Chalsa. These two approaches are through Indian territory and India can deploy its forces to guard these routes. The third route is through Doklam Plateau – Samtse District of Bhutan – Nagarkata/Banarhat/Birpara. This route passes through Bhutan and Indian Army cannot deploy any forces there. This route is very difficult to defend and NH 17 is likely to fall to the Chinese early in the war. If Chinese use this approach, there could be a large number of Bhutanese refugees who will come into India. There are three main roads which connect NH 17 and NH 27. Western most is Chalsa – Lataguri – Mainaguri; Binnaguri – Gairkata – Dhupguri and Birpara – Falakata. The approaches from North Bangladesh into this sector are Lalmonirhat – Patgram – Nagar Chandrabandha – Mainaguri and Lalmonir Hat – Sitalkuchi – Mathabhanga – Falakata. The entire area is a riverine plain. Defences will have to be based on built-up areas or minor water obstacles. This area is the most vulnerable as it can be attacked from the north by the Chinese and from the south by Bangladesh.

Area between Torsa and Rydak Rivers. The Torsa River originates in Bhutan and flows into India west of Phuntsholing, the gateway to Bhutan – west of Hashimara – west and south of Coochbehar. The main towns in the area are Cooch Behar and Alipurduar. NH 17 turns south at Birpara and runs through Falakat – Sonarpur – Cooch Behar – Assam. NH 27 runs through Alipurduar – Gosaingaon – Guwahati. There is one main link between the two, road Cooch Behar – Alipurduar. The terrain to the north of NH 27 is mostly tea gardens. The area south of NH 27 is mainly paddy fields. Chinese can reach this sector through the Samtse – Phuntsholing Highway. However, this is unlikely as the Highway passes through high mountain range and would be difficult to provide adequate artillery support. However, a diversionary attack by a small force cannot be ruled out. The main approach to this area from Bangladesh is Lalmonirhat – Dharla Bridge – Phulbari – Dinahata – Coochbehar. Since a link up with the Chinese is difficult, this approach could only be for a diversionary attack or to capture some territory for bargaining purpose.

Northern Bangladesh. (Map 3).

The Chinese can attack the Siliguri Corridor through Chumbi Valley/ Yadong County but cannot maintain forces there over the Himalayas during monsoon and winter seasons. Hence, they cannot cut off Siliguri Corridor without help from Bangladesh. They need Bangladesh to attack the Siliguri Corridor with two to three divisions and provide logistic support to troops holding the Corridor. North Bangladesh borders the Siliguri Corridor. India has a 500 km border with Northern Bangladesh extending from Farraka in West Bengal to Golakganj in Assam. Hence, knowing the terrain, road system and army locations in Northern Bangladesh is important.

Terrain. The terrain in Northern Bangladesh is generally flat with no major water obstacles.

Road Network. There is an excellent network of roads in the area. National Highways connect Takurgaon and Dinajpur to Rangpur and Bogra. Bogra to Siliguri is 284 kms. The National Highway network connects Bogra to Dhaka which is 191 kms. Dhaka holds one infantry division and one armoured brigade. There are numerous district and village roads. The routes into the Siliguri Corridor have already been discussed. There are numerous roads that lead in India and these can be easily seen on a Google Map.

Cantonments. 11 Infantry Division is located at Bogra. 93rd Armoured Brigade, 5th East Bengal Regiment, 26 Infantry Brigade, 11 Infantry Brigade are all located there. 11 Artillery Brigade is located at Jahangirabad. 66 Infantry Division is located at Rangpur. 7th Horse Regiment, 72 Infantry Brigade, and 34th Bangladesh Infantry Regiment are located at Rangpur; 66th Artillery Brigade and 16 Infantry Brigade are at Kholahat; 222nd Infantry Brigade is at Saidpur.

Chinese Activities in Yadong Country and Bhutan.

Source: eurasiatimes.com/header-china-has-bult-22-villages). China has annexed the areas of Bhutan which it claims and has built 22 villages and settlements in the annexed areas. Seven of these cross-border constructions have come up since early 2023. According to a report by 'Turquoise Roof' – a network of Tibetan analysts, satellite imagery shows around 752 residential blocks, housing an estimated 2,284 family-sized units. Approximately 7,000 people are being relocated to these previously unpopulated areas. All these villages are linked by roads to Chinese towns in Yadong County. In 2021, China constructed a village in territory claimed by India, naming it "Luoba (Lhoba) New Village." This village is located in an area that was seized from Indian control by Chinese troops in 1959, just before the 1962 Indo-Chinese War. Since then, China has maintained full control over that territory. These villages provide bases for China for gaining control of the Doklam Plateau. The southern ridge (Zompelri) at Doklam overlooks the strategically vital Siliguri Corridor, which connects mainland India to its northeastern provinces.

Analysis.

China will attack the Siliguri Corridor in the Central sector. Bangladesh will attack in the western and central sectors. Link up between the two thrusts can take place at Sevoke, Teesta Barrage or Teesta Bridge on NH 27.

Relative Strength

China. Tibet Military District has the equivalent of one division in Shigatse Region and one border guard regiment at Yadong. 77th Group Army could bring in another two divisions. **Bangladesh** has two infantry divisions and one armoured brigade. It could bring in one additional division and an armoured brigade from Dhaka. Combined, the two countries could deploy up to six divisions and two armoured brigades against Sikkim, and the Siliguri Corridor which has about 100 km of border with Samtse District of Bhutan and about 150 km of border with Bangladesh,

India. To defend Sikkim and the Siliguri Corridor, from information available on open source, India has XXXIII Corps with three divisions and no armour.

Analysis. In my opinion, XXXIII is not in a position to defend the Siliguri Corridor and Sikkim against an attack by combined force of China and Bangladesh. India needs to induct two infantry divisions and one armoured brigade to defend the Siliguri Corridor from attack by Bangladesh and China.

Time and Space

Campaign Season. There are two campaign seasons in the Himalayas; summer 15 Mar to 15 Jun and autumn 15 Oct to 15 Dec. In the plains of North Bengal and Bangladesh, the campaign season extends throughout the year except the monsoon which is from 15 Jun to 15 Oct.

Time for Buildup. China has stockpiled its operational requirements around Yadong. Bangladesh cantonments are within 50 kms from the border. Thus, "Cold Start" or launching operations without large scale mobilization is possible. Small scale mobilizations in the name of "Tactical Exercise with Troops would be normal.

Duration of the Campaign. This will depend on India's defence preparedness in the Siliguri Corridor. If present state of preparedness continues, the war could be over in two weeks with the area firmly in Chinese/Bangladeshi control. Recapturing the area could take years.

Summary

Enemy Aim and Intensions. Pakistan's animosity towards India stems from Kashmir and need to avenge humiliation of 1971 defeat. China's animosity stems from claim on Arunachal and presence of Dalai Lama. Bangladesh animosity is presence of Sheikh Hasina and deportation of immigrants and border trade restrictions. All three would love to get together and dismember India at an opportune moment.

Terrain. China is likely to attack from Doklam Plateau in the corridor between Teesta and Torsa Rivers. Bangladesh could attack on seven approaches; Thakurgaon- Goalpukur - Kishenganj; Thakurgaon -Barakhanti -Islampur; Thkurgaon -Panchagarh -Siliguri; Thakurgaon -Boda- Haldibari -Jalpaiguri, Lalmonirhat – Patgram – Nagar Chandrabandha – Mainaguri and Lalmonir Hat – Sitalkuchi – Mathabhanga – Falakata, Lalmonirhat – Dharla Bridge – Phulbari – Dinahata – Coochbehar.

Relative Strength. China and Bangladesh can attack India with three divisions each, supported by two armoured brigades, one mechanized brigade and at least three artillery brigades. XXXIII Corps of India is not in a position to defend the Siliguri Corridor against a combined attack by China and Bangladesh. India needs to induct two infantry divisions and at least one armoured brigade to ensure security of the Siliguri Corridor.

Analysis

It is unlikely that China will attempt this operation unless it is sure of success. I visualize four contingencies for them to attempt to dismember India.

The first situation is if Chinese Navy and Indian Navy as a part of the US led QUAD clash in the Pacific Ocean or South China Sea.

The second situation is if there is a World War III and India sides with the US.

The third contingency is if the separatist movements in India, particularly in the North East cause a serious situation in the country and thereby provide China and opportunity to take Arunachal Pradesh.

The fourth contingency is if India attacks Pakistan as a response to Pahalgam terrorist attack, China and Bangladesh may attack Siliguri Corridor to help Pakistan and seize the opportunity to get Arunachal.

However, I would like to re-quote Sun Tzu's famous lines, *"The art of war teaches us not to rely on the likelihood of the enemy not coming, but on our readiness to receive him: not on the chance of his not attacking but rather on the fact that we have made our position unassailable."*

CHAPTER NINE

Making of a General

"The personality of the general is indispensable. He is the head; he is the all of an army. The Gaul's were not conquered by the Roman Legions but by Caesar. It was not before the Carthaginian soldier that Rome was made to tremble, but before Hannibal. It was not the Macedonian phalanx which penetrated India but Alexander. Prussia was not defended for seven years against the three most formidable European powers by Prussian soldiers but by Frederick the Great". - Napoleon

History has proved again and again that no matter how large and supposedly powerful any armed forces may be, they can accomplish little without accomplished leaders. Babar defeated the hordes of Ibrahim Lodi at Panipat. Frederick the Great repeatedly defeated forces having twice his strength. General O'Conner defeated numerically superior Italian forces in North Africa in the First Libyan Campaign and General McArthur turned defeat into victory at Inchon. General Omar Bradley said "Man for man, one division is as good as another, they vary on the skill and leadership of their commanders". The same is true for any brigade or battalion. The essential traits and character qualities of senior commanders thus merit detailed study so that selection and development of potential commanders can be more effective.

Military life and work, by its nature, is full of contradictions. On one hand, the fact that a large number of men have to live and work together requires imposition of strict discipline under which they have to conform to well defined codes of conduct and function in a particular manner. On the other hand, the fluid nature of mechanized warfare, counter insurgency operations or air land battle calls for initiative, understanding and critical judgment, all these being the antithesis of conformity and authoritarianism. The peace time environment in the armed forces encourage the breeding of senior commanders who stick to rules, always conform to the wishes of their superiors, and sacrifice their independence of action by first ascertaining the preference of his superiors on which to base his conduct. Peace time tends to produce anti-intellectualism because intellectualism is seen as anti-establishment. Thus Colonel (later Major General) F C Fuller of the British Army was denied the permission to write a book. Capt. B H Little Hart, the well-known author of military sciences was forced to retire. So was General Percy Hobart, one of the earliest authorities on tank warfare. It is also necessary to guard against this syndrome by which officers like Lieutenant General B M Kaul rise to the top. This can only be achieved if the authorities have a clear understanding as to what goes into the making of a great general.

Role of a Commander

The role of any commander in battle is to defeat his enemy. To achieve victory in war, the commander has to be able to do the following:

Motivate his command to give their best.

Integrate all elements of his command into a homogeneous and effective force.

Train his command to a fine pitch so that they can out-perform the enemy.

Out think, outwit, and out manoeuvre his enemy so that he can bring to bear the full potential of his force into battle while preventing the enemy from doing so.

Motivating the Command

The will to fight is perhaps the most important battle winning factor. General G S Patton has aptly summed this by saying, "Wars are fought with weapons, but they are won by men. It is the spirit of the men who follow and the man who leads that gains victory." In my book, "Outstanding Victories of the Indian Army," we have seen the effect of the leadership of Major R S Dayal, Lt Col Tarapore, Major Hoshiar Singh, to name a few, on the outcome of battle. There are many factors which motivate men like good weapon systems, numerical and technological superiority, and adequacy of resources. But the most important factor is the leader himself. Napoleon, Slim, McArthur led defeated troops to victory. The traits and character qualities which enable a commander to motivate his command are honour, courage, confidence, benevolence, sincerity, own morale, and determination.

Integrating the Command

The importance of integrating all elements of one's command on the modern battle field with its plethora of weapon systems and support systems is a challenging task. General Guderian was a master of the art and his Panzer forces highlighted the effectiveness of combined arms operations. We have also seen how the ability of 54 Infantry Division to integrate mine breaching trawals with their Engineers enabled them to use them effectively to breach the mine field at Basantar, whereas 39 Infantry Division failed and lost their trawls. The concept is nothing new. Cooperation is one of the principles of war. The character qualities which enable a commander to integrate his forces are knowledge, vision, wisdom, objectivity, listening capability, perspective, and patience.

Training the Command

Training is a battle winning factor. Frederick the Great could defeat forces superior in number because his troops could shoot three times faster than the enemy and march quicker. The Romans could build their empire because of superior battle drills of the Roman Legions. Our own armoured regiments equipped with the out-dated Sherman and Centurion tanks won handsome victories at Assal Uttar, Phillora and Basantar over the superior Patton tanks mainly because of superior training. The character qualities which enable a commander to train his command effectively are vision, strictness, persuasion, and determination.

Out Witting the Enemy

Surprise is one of the most fundamental principles of war which has been stressed from Sun Tsu to the most modern military thinker. Hannibal's attack across the Alps, Mohammed II's ferrying of ships across land, the Normandy and Inchon landings have all highlighted the importance of surprise. Our own victories at Zoji La, Rajauri, Bayra, Dacca etc were largely due to our ability to surprise the enemy. Commanders who have successfully out thought, out witted and out manoeuvred the enemy were all creative people. These great captains of war had character qualities like creativity, vision, conceptual ability, intuition, perspective and a high-risk profile or boldness.

Essential Character Qualities and Traits

Having discussed the role of a commander and the character qualities necessary to carry out these roles, let us delve a little in the character qualities themselves.

Honour

George Washington said, "War must be carried out systematically and to do it you must have men of character activated by the principles of honour." Senior commanders must be standard bearers and must abide by the highest standards of conduct and selfless service. The concept of honour is complex. However, in essence it prompts trust and professional commitment. Some essential qualities of honourable men are enumerated below.

Honesty

Commanders have to be honest. Honesty is difficult to define. There is a fine line between perks of office and misappropriation of government funds. There is no need to forego the perks of office to be honest. At the same time, taking away mess or regimental property, use of regimental funds for purchase private items or not paying mess bills will hardly enhance the image of commanders. Honesty is necessary not only in financial terms but also in dealings. Honesty in performance appraisal, examining merits and demerits of plans and problems is equally important. Favouritism must be consciously avoided.

Truthfulness

A man of deceit, who forgets his commitments as soon as he leaves the scene, who makes false promises and gains cheap popularity can never enjoy the trust of his command.

Selflessness

A leader whose actions are motivated by considerations of career advancement or personal gains are easily seen through by their command and thus never enjoy their trust. Alexander's pouring a glass of water offered on to the sand in front of his thirsty soldiers did wonders for their morale. General Manekshaw's offer to resign rather than launch offensive against East Pakistan in April 1971 is a shining example of moral courage and selflessness.

Dependability

Troops willingly follow a commander on whom they can depend, whom they can trust. It goes without saying that example is more important than precept. Faith, trust and admiration are feelings which the command must feel for their commanders. The great captains of war were without exception were honourable men.

Courage

Courage is of two types, physical courage or gallantry and moral courage to stand up for their beliefs and convictions. Both are essential for commanders.

Physical Courage

Physical courage to face danger alongside the troops is an essential trait in successful senior commanders. Napoleon, Rommel, Patton and Slim to mention a few and our own Lieutenant Generals Sagat Singh, Ranjit Singh Dayal and Z A Bakshi displayed it in great measure. It is interesting to note what General L K Truscott, US Army, had to say about the defeat of American forces by Rommel at Kasserine Pass; "One contributing factor to American reverses was the command method of most of the American commanders, who conducted their battles from a command post which they seldom left. Few commanders in higher echelons ever spent much time in personal reconnaissance, visiting troops or inspecting dispositions.

Moral Courage

This form of courage is perhaps the hardest to come by but is most important in senior commanders. It involves disagreement with superiors and at times disobedience of orders which are likely to be seen as a breach of discipline or disloyalty and result in death or dishonour. It requires supreme confidence, an iron will, fine judgment and perhaps a bit of luck for stands based on moral courage to succeed. However, many battles have been won and many lives saved by creative disobedience or insubordination. It is interesting to note that Nelson's victory at Trafalgar was achieved by violating the naval doctrines and for which other admirals had been shot. At the battle of Zondor in 1758, Frederick the Great ordered his cavalry commander General Frederick Von Seydlith to charge Russian guns. The order was thrice refused with the reply, "After the battle the king can do what he likes with my head, but during the battle he may please allow me to use it". Nearer home, General Manekshaw refused the dictates of Mrs Indira Gandhi to launch the offensive into East Pakistan in April 1971 and offered to resign. The resignation of General Sardeshpande over the issue of authorization of married accommodation to IPKF troops posted at Madras is another shining though less publicized example.

Confidence

"A good military leader must dominate the events which encompass him; once events get the better of him, he will lose the confidence of his men and when that happens, he ceases to be of value as a leader", thus spoke Field Marshal Montgomery. A leader must always appear confident and in control of the situation. Confidence comes from his own competence, a thorough understanding of the capabilities of his men and weapon systems, foresight, decisiveness, and courage. A commander must be unflappable and always cool. Lack of confidence is extremely contagious and can lead to a rout. The role of General Harbaksh Singh, GOC in C Western Command, in restoring the morale of the officers and men of 4 Mountain Division after their disastrous performance at Khemkaran on September 6, 1965 turned defeat into victory in the Battle of Assal Uttar that followed. It is interesting to note that the Corps Commander had recommended that the formation be replaced and four of the six battalions be immediately disbanded. The confidence of General Sparrow in the 7 Cavalry carried the day at Zoji La.

Benevolence

A senior commander must always have the well-being of his men at heart. Frederick the Great cautioned all senior leaders and commanders to care for their soldiers. He said, "The commander should appear friendly to his soldiers, speak to them on the march, visit them while they are cooking, ask them if they are well cared for and alleviate their needs if they have any." Lieutenant General P S Bhagat, Victoria Cross died in the early seventies. He is still remembered by many for the interest he took in making the lives of soldiers under his command and that of their families more bearable.

Vision or Perspective

All actions start with a vision, a clear-cut idea or perspective of what we want to achieve. In simple words, a commander must know how to set and achieve goals. No coherent battle or campaign plan can be fought without a lucid vision of how it is to be fought or concluded. Vision or the ability to see the future, to be able to read the battle through the fog of war, to be able to identify the weaknesses of the enemy and how to exploit it, to be able to assess the effects of social, economic, and technological changes on warfare is a senior officer's source of effectiveness. A senior leader must have the ability to visualize the enemy's pattern of operations and formulate his own concept of operations. Clarity of thinking and intuitive sensing are important inputs into vision. Foresight is another complementary quality. It is this clarity of vision which enabled the Indian Army to relive Leh in 1948 and capture Dacca in 1971. Lack of the same resulted in disaster in 1962, failure to reinforce Zoji La in May 1948 and stalemate and needless casualties in IPKF operations in Sri Lanka.

Wisdom

Wisdom is the ability to do the right thing as against doing a thing right. It calls for great depth of knowledge not only about tactics and strategies of war but also about human nature and an awareness of the political, economic and environmental situation. It calls for the ability to see problems in their long-term and true perspective. It requires calmness of temper and serenity of mind. It requires a commander to rise above ego problems, regimental, and other petty loyalties, and be devoted to the nation, to the service and to the men. It calls for uprightness of character and objectivity in decision making.

Creativity

The basic instrument of military creativity is creative decision making. The first characteristic of creativity is originality. General J C Fuller observes: "Originality, not conventionality is one of the main pillars of "generalship". To do something that the enemy does not expect, is not prepared for, something that will surprise him and disarm him morally. To spy out the soul of one's adversary, to act in a manner which will astonish and bewilder him, this is "generalship". . This is the foundation of success". The sure test of military creativity is the surprise it causes on the enemy. Classic Indian examples are the Battle of Shalateng, 1947, Battle of Zojila, 1948 and the capture of Dacca.

Another characteristic of creativity is that it integrates ideas and technological advances into the concept of war. The British first introduced the tank to the battlefield in 1918 but it was the Germans who successfully integrated them into and effective fighting machine in the form of their Panzer Divisions. The concept of the air land battle, so successfully used in the Gulf War, is another example of military creativity. Bridging of Madhumati River in Bangladesh by a combination of Folding Boat Equipment and Bailey Bridge Equipment, crossing of the Meghna without conventional river crossing equipment, use of assault lanes and selective mine breaching in the Battle of Basantar are excellent examples of military creativity of the Indian Army. The ingredients of military creativity are listed below.

Intellectual Ability

The intellect operates through five faculties: cognition, memory, vertical or logical thinking and evaluation. Cognition is the action of knowing. It includes formation of ideas and perception. Lateral or non-logical thinking is the faculty by which the mind can think in different directions in its attempt to find answers to problems which are capable of a variety of solutions. This is the ability which produces original ideas. Evaluation is the ability of the mind which after considering the relevant factors of the problem is able to come to a decision as to correctness, suitability, or workability of the solution.

Problem Sensitivity

A problem can be tackled effectively provided it is understood in its true perspective. The cadre review has been unable to solve the problem of stagnation but created a host of others like changing the primacy from command to staff. A creative commander must be able to see a problem in its correct perspective.

Fluency of Ideas

A creative person has more ideas at a time than non-creative persons. Memory and non-logical thinking are the key to fluency of ideas.

Flexibility in Thinking

This trait enables the thinker to keep attacking problems with a variety of techniques and also redefining the problem or aim. General Sato, the Commander of Japanese forces lost a great opportunity of winning the war through inflexibility by wasting vital time in capturing Kohima when the route to Dimapur lay undefended in front his troops. Rommel said that no plan survives beyond the first day of battle. To win, commanders must have the flexibility to change plans as required to achieve the ultimate aim. Operations of 4 Corps in the Bangladesh War of 1971 is a good example of flexibility in battle.

Originality

Originality is a produce of non-logical thinking and evaluation. A creative person is not afraid of being unconventional. As discussed earlier, originality is an essential quality of "generalship". Unfortunately, most schools of instruction discourage originality. It can be said without fear of contradiction that all great military leaders like Hannibal, Alexander, Rommel, Von Manstien, McArthur, Patton, Guderian and Frederick the Great were creative thinkers.

High Risk-Taking Profile or Boldness

Risk taking means taking needed decisions in varied degrees of uncertainty. Risk taking does not mean gambling. Risks are only justified when it will further the aim or goal. Risks are also necessary for an outnumbered force. An excellent example is General O'Conner's attack on the Italian forces in North Africa, where, what started as a spoiling attack led to complete defeat of the Italians and capture of more prisoners than the attacking force. The Battle of Shalateng, 1947 is another example. It is unrealistic to expect a clear and complete picture during war for decision making. Inaction and neglect of fleeting tactical opportunities are disastrous. Higher commanders must have offensive spirit and a high-risk taking profile. This is not possible in an environment where mistakes are not acceptable and golf and mess functions need to be rehearsed.

Conceptual Ability

Montgomery said, "The acid test of an officer who aspires to high command is his ability to grasp quickly the essentials of a military problem." Conceptual ability enables a commander to do this and establish long-term and short-term goals. Conceptual skill requires common sense, vision, creativity, intuition, judgment, imagination, and a clear understanding of the principles of war and basic considerations of the various operation of war. Those who lack conceptual skills typically pursue short term goals without regard to long term consequence. The emphasis is on form over substance, minor staff duties over major staff duties, on the cover instead of the contents. 4 Mountain Divisions involvement in Khustia, 9 Infantry Divisions pursuit of enemy to Khulna and 1 Corps operations in the Shakargarh Bulge in 1971 illustrates the point.

Determination

Senior commanders must be men of iron will. They must not give up but pursue the objective relentlessly. Battles are always lost in the hearts and mind before they are actually lost. The debacle at Sela and the fall of the Fortress Singapore are some examples of military disasters brought on by lack of determination in commanders.

Training

Senior commanders can only succeed if their armies are well trained. Commanders must therefore demand and accept the highest standards of training. Training is only possible if resources and time is provided. Unrealistic training instructions and training on paper can lead to disaster.

Patience

A senior commander has to integrate diverse personalities and forces into a well-knit fighting team. To achieve this, he needs patience and tact, firmness and persuasiveness and good powers of listening. He must patiently listen to his subordinates and encourage them to speak up and come out with suggestions.

Undesirable Qualities

Having said much about the desirable qualities and traits of senior commanders, it would be appropriate to touch upon a few undesirable traits which need to be eradicated. These are careerism, egoism, indecisiveness, and hypocrisy.

Careerism

This is a trait which puts self before service. To the careerist, the honour and welfare of the boss comes first, always and every time; his own honour and welfare comes next and all else comes last always and every time. A careerist does not believe in long-term objectives. He concentrates on what he can achieve during his tenure and what will please his boss. He believes in spit, polish, parties, and golf as important props to career advancement. Careerism is the antithesis of professionalism.

Egoism

Egoism is the trait in a commander which makes him feel that he is the know all and be all of everything. He cannot tolerate contrary views which in other words means professionalism. He enjoys flattery, sycophancy and the five-star culture. He cannot stand any moralistic or professional stand. When his ego is hurt, he becomes angry and becomes vindictive. Egoism is the antithesis of wisdom.

Indecisiveness

Many commanders avoid decision making. They are forever asking for comments and views and trying to ascertain what reply or action the superiors would like to be taken. They have no convictions. They are afraid to make a mistake or to offend superiors. Indecisiveness can be fatal in a battle. Fleeting tactical opportunities can only be exploited by bold commanders. Delay in decisions making gives the enemy time to reorganize and regroup. Indecisiveness is the antithesis of courage and confidence.

Hypocrisy

The hypocrite preaches morality, high ideals and impeccable conduct but practices the opposite. He insists on a mess bill but blows his top if the bill exceeds Rs 10 per meal or some such paltry sum. He talks of economy in use of transport but uses the staff car to go for golf. He talks of austerity but expects Scotch whiskey, lavish food, and silver mementos. Hypocrisy is the antithesis of honour and sincerity.

Summary

The peace time environment in the armed forces encourage the breeding of senior commanders who stick to rules, always conform to the wishes of their superiors, and sacrifice their independence of action. Peace time tends to produce anti-intellectualism because intellectualism is seen as anti-establishment.

Role of a Commander in battle is to defeat his enemy. To achieve victory in war, the commander has to be able to motivate his command to give their best; integrate all elements of his command into a homogeneous and effective force; train his command to a fine pitch so that they can out-perform the enemy; out think, outwit and out manoeuvre his enemy so that he can bring to bear the full potential of his force into battle while preventing the enemy from doing so.

Desirable traits of commanders are honesty, selflessness, dependability, confidence, vision, physical courage, moral courage, wisdom, benevolence, creativity, problem sensitivity, flexibility in thinking, originality, conceptual ability, boldness, determination, patience, and training.

Undesirable traits of commanders are careerism, egoism, indecisiveness, and hypocrisy.

"Thus. we may know that there are five essentials for victory: 1. He (the general) will win who knows when to fight and when not to fight.

2. He will win who knows how to handle both superior and inferior forces.

3. He will win whose army is animated by the same spirit throughout all its ranks.

4. He will win who, prepared himself, waits to take the enemy unprepared.

5. He will win who has military capacity and is not interfered with by the sovereign." — Sun Tzu, The Art of War

Conclusion

"The personality of the general is indispensable. He is the head; he is the all of an army. The Gaul's were not conquered by the Roman Legions but by Caesar. It was not before the Carthaginian soldier that Rome was made to tremble, but before Hannibal. It was not the Macedonian phalanx which penetrated India but Alexander. Prussia was not defended for seven years against the three most formidable European powers by Prussian soldiers but by Frederick the Great". - Napoleon

History has proved again and again that no matter how large and supposedly powerful any armed forces may be, they can accomplish little without accomplished leaders. Napoleon said, "It is exceptional and difficult to find in one man all the qualities of a great general. That which is most desirable and which instantly sets a man apart is that his intelligence is balanced by his character and courage". Rommel said, "A commander's drive and energy counts for more than his personal power". It is also a fact that without creative thinking, no victory is possible.

It is a truism that no matter how large or powerful any armed forces may be, they can accomplish little without competent leaders. Different great captains of war had different dominating traits. Genghis Khan relied on speed of manoeuvre and ruthlessness, Nelson on audacity, Rommel on speed and opportunism, Hannibal on audacity and deception, Montgomery on methodical preparation. The list can go on. But certain qualities they had in common. They were all men of character and honour. They were men of vision. They were creative men who were able to train and integrate their armies into well knit, effective fighting machines who would follow their leaders unto death. These are the character qualities and traits which all senior commanders must acquire.

Kashmir was saved in 1947 by Brigadier LP Sen. Better armed Pakistan Army was defeated by General Harbaksh Singh in 1965. Field Marshal Manekshaw, General Aurora and General Sagat Singh liberated East Pakistan in 17 days in one of the most remarkable victories of all times. Who do we have now to lead the armed forces? Those well versed in the art and principles of war or those who are well versed in the art and principles of managing seniors; a Manekshaw, or a BM Kaul?

CHAPTER TEN

Suggested Action Plan

It is a little presumptuous on my part to suggest an action plan to improve our readiness for war to the Government of India and our esteemed political leaders and generals of the armed forces. These are mere humble suggestions from an 84-year-old soldier, waiting his turn to join the que for rebirth; an old soldier who loves his country and the army which is his family, and does not want to see a repeat of the 1962 debacle.

For Government of India

Battlefield Surveillance. India should launch geo-stationary satellites over Chumbi Valley, Northern Bangladesh, Chinese /Tibetan areas opposite Arunachal Pradesh and ensure dedicated day to day monitoring of military activities in these areas. The US and Israel can pick up individual vehicles carrying suspected terrorists. India should be able to pick up military movements and troop concentrations.

At least double the defence budget for defence acquisitions, DRDO and operational readiness. The money can be found from reducing budget allocation to NHAI and High-Speed Rail projects.

Increasing Government Income

The government should increase revenue by the undermentioned methods.

Introducing a transaction tax of 0.01% on Stock exchanges. Increase in price of cigarettes or liquor does not stop people from smoking or drinking. People with money will spend on whatever they want irrespective of cost. People pay millions for space tourism. Singapore has this tax.

Increase Tax on Vehicles. Make tax on new vehicles costing over Rs 5 lakhs 100%. This will reduce number of new vehicles which in turn will reduce congestion, pollution, and parking problems. Rich will still buy. Singapore has this tax.

Strengthen the Rupee. To reduce the demand for foreign currency for non-essential requirements, put 20% tax on conversion of Rupee into foreign exchange for any purpose other than purchase of industrial inputs and medical equipment. A strong Rupee will reduce the cost of purchase of weapons and crude oil.

Encourage Savings. Savings in fixed deposits and RBI bonds will make it easier for the Government to borrow. Make interest on all fixed deposits and RBI bonds tax free.

Produce Drones. It should Initiate action on priority to develop and produce in large numbers low-cost Kamikaze drones for hitting enemy targets like armour, fuel depots, ammunition depots, troop concentrations etc.

Reduce Dependence on imported crude oil. India needs to reduce its vulnerability to increase in oil prices or disruption in crude oil supplies due to war. This is to be done in two ways.

Increasing Domestic Production. India must provide adequate funds to ONGC and OIL for new drilling and production. Relying on Private Sector investment is not effective. The state of production from Barmer field in Rajasthan is one example.

Introducing Mini Nuclear Plants. India must introduce mini nuclear plants to produce electricity using the technology used in nuclear powered ships and submarines. Since nuclear plant need a lot of water and land, these mini nuclear plants can set up on the banks of large lakes and reservoirs like Dal Lake in Kashmir, Hirakud Dam in Odisha, all over the country. These projects will require little land acquisition, less investment, less gestation time and cause little damage to environment. Small Modular reactors are commercially available. One company is Rolls Royce SMR Ltd.

Strengthen Defence PSUs. I congratulate Modiji for converting the Ordnance Factories into Defence PSUs. That is not enough. These PSUs need to be strengthened by infusing working capital, giving orders, and inducting CEOs from Private Sector.

Economise Defence Expenditure

This should be the responsibility of the Armed Forces. But, the various components of the armed forces are very protective of their empires and would not by themselves ever suggest measures to reduce personnel or operations. Many of the practices followed in the armed forces are rooted in our colonial past. Modiji has got the IPC revised. He may also like to push some reforms in line with a developed India. Kindly note that I can only suggest reforms for the army in which I served for 28 years. Also, kindly note that I retired in 1991, 34 years ago. Some of the reforms I suggest may already have been implemented.

Recruit only Engineering Graduates into technical Arms & Services. Only about 50 percent of officers in the Corps of Engineers, Corps of Signals and Corps of Electrical and Mechanical Engineers join the army after graduating as engineers. Others do a three-year degree course at College of Military Engineering, College of Military Telecommunication Engineering or Military College of Electrical Engineers. This was all right in the sixties when there were very few engineering colleges in the country. Today, India produces over 200,000 engineers every year. A thousand suitable candidates would certainly happily join the Army. The pay and allowances of the officers doing degree course cost the Army thousands of crores every year. Abolishing degree course for officers will also improve the availability of young officers in units by two to three. Graduate engineer entries have performed very well even in the General Cadre. Lt. Gen. Narhari not only commanded an infantry division but was also the Commandant of College of Combat.

Stop trades training at Regimental Centres in trades being taught at Government run Industrial Training Institutes and recruit directly from these.

Review the vehicle discard policy because of which vehicles which have done less than 1 lakh km are discarded.

Review India's Military Strength and Deployment. India's military capability must be based on enemy capability and not intentions. Intentions can change with the change of government. The Awami League regime in Bangladesh has been replaced by a caretaker, Pakistan friendly, government. All bon homey between India and Bangladesh has disappeared overnight and relations have soured. It is always necessary to know the military capabilities of our neighbours and to be ready for any eventuality. It is necessary to be aware of the military buildup that has taken place in Bangladesh over the last two decades. It needs to be remembered that relations between nations are not permanent. National interests are. Egypt under Nasser was anti-US and anti-Israel. Egypt under Al Sisi is pro-US and pro-Israel. Too much need not be read into statements made by politicians. The Chinese echoed Nehru's Hindi Chini Bhai Bhai and Panchsheel while annexing Aksai Chin from India. Mr. Nawaz Sharif was inducting infiltrators into Kargil while signing the Lahore Declaration. France expresses solidarity with India while selling fighter aircrafts and submarines to Pakistan. China feels that it may need India's support to stand up to a dominating United States. But relations will deteriorate if India gets too close to the United States.

Actions by the Armed Forces

Finalize Defensive Plan against attack on Siliguri Corridor. Eastern Command should immediately hold a war-game to analyse the requirements of defending the Siliguri Corridor against a combined force of one Chinese Army Group operating through Chumbi Valley and two to three divisions of Bangla Desh army attacking from the south. A Tactical Exercise With Troops should be conducted to finalize plans for construction of permanent defences to ensure speedy deployment when necessary. At least two divisions and one armoured brigade should be moved from western sector to the eastern sector. A new Corps Headquarters should be raised for the defence of the Siliguri Corridor.

Address Officer Shortage. There is a shortfall of 7799 Officers and 108685 Soldiers in the Indian Army; 1446 Officers and 12151 Sailors in the Indian Navy; and 572 Officers and 5217 Airmen in the Indian Air Force. During the years 2020 & 2021. (Source: www.digitalsansad.in). This amounts to about 20% of the authorized strength. This is suicidal. The Army must start filling up shortage of young officers by reintroducing Emergency Commission in batches of 800 officers every three months. Even at this rate, it will take two and half years to get to full strength.

Abolish "Agniveer" scheme. The "Agniveer" Scheme of recruiting four-year contract soldiers is not suited for the arms i.e. Armoured Corps, Infantry, Artillery, Engineers, and Signals because the operations of these arms require the motivation of regimental spirit and years of collective training and bonding. This recruitment must stop. The scheme can be used for recruiting men for the services like Army Supply Corps, Electrical and Mechanical Engineers and Ordnance Corps who operate behind the front lines and rarely engage in combat.

Start regular recruitment of jawans with the aim of reaching authorized strength in one year's time. The shortage of over one lakh soldiers will prove to be a disaster if war breaks out. The strength is going down every month as retirement continues. It takes a minimum of six months to train a jawan and another six months at least for him to find his feet in his battalion or regiment.

Start Passive Defence Activities. India is a vast country. It is not economically possible to provide adequate air defence capability to all vulnerable areas and points. Even Israel, which arguably has the best air defence capability, has underground air bases, hospitals, and command centres. India must immediately start preparing underground command centres, ammunition depots, fuel storage tanks and shelters for troops and even civilians.

Summary

The author has humbly suggested an action plan for the Government of India and Armed Forces for kind considerations of the Authorities. They mainly pertain to the Army because the author has served 28 years in the army and has first-hand knowledge of problems.

Actions by the Government

Battlefield Surveillance. India should launch geo-stationary satellites over Chumbi Valley, Northern Bangladesh, Chinese /Tibetan areas opposite Arunachal Pradesh and ensure dedicated day to day monitoring of military activities in these areas.

At least double the defence budget for defence acquisitions, DRDO and operational readiness. The money can be found from reducing budget allocation to NHAI and High-Speed Rail projects.

Increasing Government Income

Introducing a transaction tax of 0.01% on Stock exchanges. Increase in price of cigarettes or liquor does not stop people from smoking or drinking. Singapore has this tax.

Increase Tax on Vehicles. Make tax on new vehicles costing over Rs 5 lakhs 100%. Singapore has this tax.

Strengthen the Rupee. To reduce the demand for foreign currency for non-essential requirements, put 20% tax on conversion of Rupee into foreign exchange for any purpose other than purchase of industrial inputs and medical equipment.

Encourage Savings. Savings in fixed deposits and RBI bonds will make it easier for the Government to borrow. Make interest on all fixed deposits and RBI bonds tax free.

Increase India's Defence Production. India can produce rockets which launch satellites, ships, and nuclear submarines. India can send a rocket to the moon. Why can it not produce tanks, artillery pieces, helicopters, and fighter aircraft? Why is the Defence Research and Development Organization (DRDO) unable to develop the equipment we require and produce the same?

Qualitative Requirements (QR). The main reason is the QR for weapon systems which is drawn up by the service headquarters. Our generals and bureaucrats do not encourage indigenous development of military equipment. The defence ministry must Form Committees under the Chairmanship of the Scientific Advisor to GOI for reviewing or formulating Qualitative Requirements (QR) for tanks, artillery, drones etc to make their indigenous production possible with available technology.

Review India's Military Strength and Deployment. India's military capability must be based on enemy capability and not intentions. Intentions can change with the change of government. All bon homey between India and Bangladesh has disappeared. Bangladesh can collude with China and Pakistan in a conflict. It is always necessary to know the military capabilities of our neighbours and to be ready for any eventuality.

Produce Drones. It should Initiate action on priority to develop and produce in large numbers low-cost Kamikaze drones for hitting enemy targets like armour, fuel depots, ammunition depots, troop concentrations etc.

Develop anti-drone and anti-missile defence. It must develop low-cost anti drone and missile defences and deploy them at vulnerable areas and vulnerable point.

Strengthen Defence PSUs by infusing working capital, giving orders, and inducting CEOs from Private Sector.

Reduce Dependence on imported crude oil by increasing domestic production and introducing Mini Nuclear Plants.

Recruit only engineering graduates into the Corps of Engineers, Corps of Signals and Corps of Electrical and Mechanicals and close engineering degree courses in the army. This will save thousands of crores and improve availability of young officers in units.

Stop trades training at Regimental Centres in trades being taught at Government run Industrial Training Institutes and recruit directly from these.

Review the vehicle discard policy because of which vehicles which have done less than 1 lakh km are discarded.

The Government should immediately form a PSU to deal with unserviceable high-value defence equipment. They should be co-located with PSUs manufacturing the equipment. Unserviceable equipment should be returned to where they are manufactured so that serviceable parts can be used and the rest disposed of.

Actions by the Armed Forces

Finalize plans for defending the Siliguri Corridor against attack by combined forces of China and Bangladesh.

Adress Shortage of Junior Officers by increasing intake. The stagnation problem for higher ranks can be solved by a system of out of turn promotion and reintroducing Emergency Commission.

Abolish "Agniveer" scheme for jawans of the Armoured Corps, Artillery, Infantry, Corps of Engineers, and Corps of Signals.

Start regular recruitment of jawans with the aim of reaching full strength in one year's time.

Economise on Defence Expenditure by reviewing outdated policies and practices. Only graduates in engineering should be recruited for technical arms and services. Trades training should stop at Regimental Centres. Vehicle discard policy needs review.

Form a Defence PSU to deal with high value defence equipment like tanks and artillery guns.

Start Passive Air Defence Activities. All headquarters, ammunition dumps, fuel dumps, and other vulnerable locations must be moved underground as early as possible.

Conclusion

Defence Expenditure is not a holy cow. A poor country like India must make sure that every penny is well spent. There are many things that can be done to make defence expenditure cost effective. However, senseless measures like the "Agniveer" recruitment are suicidal as it will destroy regimental spirit and fighting capability of the fighting arms. Nothing should be done which affects the morale and training of the man behind the gun. No battle can be won without well trained and well-motivated troops and motivated young officers. **Please do not try to save on pensions and money by not filling vacancies of young officers and soldiers. If you do so, India will lose every battle and be fragmented.**

Epilogue

I was a 22-year-old final year engineering student of Kolkata University when Chinese attacked India in October 1962. I vividly remember my grandmother, mother and aunts giving some of their gold ornaments to Government of India because the Government had no money to buy weapons. I remember them knitting sweaters and socks for jawans on the borders because the soldiers on the Himalayan borders had no warm clothing. I heard Pandit Nehru, our esteemed Prime Minister, apologizing to the people of Assam (no Arunachal or North Eastern states then) for being unable to protect them. Then the miracle happened. The Chinese Army withdrew from areas they had captured.

I joined the Indian Army as an officer in July 1963 and served till I took pre-mature retirement in 1991 as a colonel. I have seen the army at close quarters for 28 years. I have seen the good, the bad and the ugly. I have seen youthful enthusiasm of the sixties and seventies. I have seen stagnation and the rat race for promotion thereafter. I have seen the army change from a caring family to what an army commander described to me as the culture of "ACR by day and VCR by night." I have seen units staffed by full complement of daredevil young officers. I have seen units staffed by a handful of officers many of them superseded and young officers as a rare commodity. I have commanded an engineer regiment and know fully well the perils of shortage of officers and soldiers.

The hype in the media about the great and invincible Indian armed forces does not impress me. It leaves me scared. Over confidence leads to neglect. Peace time soldiering promotes rise of mediocracy and nepotism among the leadership. Unworthy generals like General B M Kaul, who was the commander of IV Corps of the Indian Army when the Chinese attacked and fled from his headquarters at Tezpur to Delhi, rise to vital appointments.

Pacifists have not learned the lessons from history. The Mauryan Empire reached its peak during the rule of Ashoka the Great. Ashoka became a pacifist after the Battle of Kalinga in 263 BCE and neglected military matters. After Ashoka died in 232 BCE, the Mauryan Empire, which stretched from Afghanistan to the Godavari River, collapsed within fifty years. Nehru was a pacifist. He led India to its most humiliating military defeat since independence. War is very much an option for nations that value their sovereignty and independence, even if it is the option of last resort. From the time of Sun Tzu (500 BCE), it is recognized that the only pragmatic and prudent approach to threat perception and defence preparedness is to go by the capability and not the intention of our possible adversaries. Intentions can change with a change of government or a head of state. And in today's violent and volatile world, governments and intentions can change overnight. But it takes tens of years and trillions of Rupees to build a credible military deterrence that will discourage our neighbours from military misadventures.

India has never fought a long war. The longest was Kashmir War 1947-48 which lasted about six months. However, the next war against China-Pakistan-Bangladesh could last much longer, especially if Siliguri Corridor is lost and has to be recaptured. India must be prepared for a long war lasting years. This requires improving production of warlike stores and ammunition and stockpiling them. It must also fill all vacancies in the armed forces and have a recruitment plan to replenish war casualties.

I believe that India must spend much more on defence. The policies and priorities of the Indian government is laid down by the economic advisor to the Government. This neoliberal economist believes in free market economy and reduction in government's role in governing India. He has no interest in seeing India as a militarily strong country. That will require a much larger defence budget and less allocation to capex in infrastructure. Let us see the budget allocation to infra projects vis a vis defence. The budget for Meerut-Delhi Rapid Rail System. 82.5 km. Cost 3.8 billion Euro or about Rs 37,000 crores. It benefits a few thousand businessmen of Delhi and Meerut. In comparison, the budget for DRDO for 2023-24 was Rs 23,264 crores. It will be seen that the budget for construction of 82 km of highspeed rail system between Delhi and Meerut is more than the budget of Defence Research and Development Organization which is supposed to develop futuristic defence system for the armed forces. It is also less than Rs 29,000 allotted to Animal Husbandry for welfare of cows.

Budget for Defence 2024-25. Rs 1.72 lakh crore allocated for capital acquisition; Rs 92,088 crore for sustenance & operational readiness. It will be seen that the allocation for sustenance and operational readiness of the armed forces is less than half of the budget for NHAI. India's defence budget needs to be at least 5% to 7% of our GDP. And most of the money must be spent in manufacturing defence needs within India and not on a few stealth aircraft or nuclear submarines.

I believe that India is in great danger. The vulnerable point is the Siliguri Corridor as explained in Chapter 8: My Threat Perception. I do not want our beloved Prime Minister apologizing to the country for being unable to protect the North-East. That is why ask the question:

IS INDIA READY FOR A LONG WAR?

Our political leaders, generals of the armed forces and the Indian Government must ensure that the answer is a big YES. The over estimation of the capabilities of the Indian Armed Forces in the electronic media is frightening and can lead to misadventure with disastrous results. India should think of going to war only when it is fully ready as it was in 1971.

I would like to again emphasize that my comments are not directed at any person or political party but made in good faith and for the good of our great nation.

About The Author

Col Bhaskar Sarkar, a graduate in civil engineering, was commissioned into the Corps of Engineers in April 1963. On completion of training, he was posted to an engineer regiment. After a three-year tenure in the regiment, he was posted as instructor Class C to College of Military Engineering. After one year, he returned to the regiment as a company commander. In this tenure he spent six months in Bhutan and built a helipad at Thimphu and took part in flood relief operation. He went as OC advance party when the regiment moved to Sagar. As Officiating CO, he was associated with planning of Exercise Betwa. His company was affiliated to an infantry brigade and took part in "Deep Thrust" exercises. In early 1971, he topped the Engineer Company Commanders Course and was posted to Tactical Wing in College of Military Engineering. A soldier by choice, he refused posting to Military Engineering Service and gave an "adverse career certificate." There, he took extra classes for degree course students and helped them pass promotion Examinations Part C and D. In 1973 he was selected to do Defence Services Staff College on a competitive vacancy and was declared reserve to do the course in Australia. After Staff College, he was posted as Brigade Major, of a Mountain Brigade engaged in insurgency operations in Nagaland. From Nagaland, Col Sarkar was posted as second in command, armoured division's engineer regiment. During this tenure, he stood first on Engineer Regimental Commander's course. Here he helped CO formulate the engineer support doctrine for the armoured division which was published as a Division's Training Instruction. Next, he was posted on the staff of 11 Corps Headquarters. Here he helped the Brigadier General Staff formulate the threat perception for 11 Corps. Col Sarkar was given command of 104 Engineer Regiment. His regiment was selected for Operation Indra Vajra, an operation to restore oil supplies to Barauni refinery from oil fields in Assam which had been stopped by the All Assam Students Union. He carried out the task with distinction and was awarded the Vishist Seva Medal. After command, Col Sarkar was selected to do Long Defence Management Course at Secundrabad. After the course he was posted as Col Q, Headquarters Eastern Command. He was awarded the Chief of Army Staff's Commendation card for his performance on the assignment. From Headquarters Eastern Command, Col Sarkar was posted as Chief Engineer Project Chetak, Border Roads on promotion to full

Colonel. After this tenure he went to College of Military Engineering as Chief Instructor, Young Officer's Wing, and later Head of Training Team in Faculty of Combat Engineering. During this tenure he was sent to Sri Lanka to study Improvised Explosive Devices used by LTTE. He also did a study on engineer support to offensive operations in the Mountains. He was passed over for promotion to Brigadier and took premature retirement.

Col Sarkar has written about 25 books and "e" books. Those related to defence matters are listed below:

Engineer Appreciations. Published in Institute of Military Engineers Journal in 1990/1991.

Pakistan Seeks Revenge and God Saves India. Published by Batra Book Service, New Delhi. Not in Print.

Tackling Insurgency and Terrorism, A Blueprint for Action. Published by Vision Books Pvt Ltd, New Delhi. Not in print.

Outstanding Victories of the Indian Army. First publishes by Lancer Publishers and Distributors, New Delhi. Republished by the author at Notion Press.com

Kargil War, Past, Present and Future. Published by Lancer Publishers and Distributors, New Delhi. Not in print.

Who is afraid of the Chinese Dragon? I am. Published by Atlantic Publishers and Distributors, New Delhi

Tackling the Naxal Problem. Published by Atlantic Publishers and Distributors, New Delhi

The World Should Help Tibetans Liberate Tibet. Self-published by Col Sarkar at Notion Press.com

His other books are listed below:

"Thirty-Nine Steps to Happiness," Atlantic Publishers and Distributors

"Introduction to Vaastu Shastra," Atlantic Publishers and Distributors

"Earthquakes: All we Need to Know About them," Atlantic Publishers and Distributors

"Introduction to Religions of the World," Atlantic Publishers and Distributors

"Nationalism: Economic Strategy for Survival of Developing Countries," Atlantic Publishers

"Occupiers of Walls Street; Losers or Game Changers." e Books available Samashwords.com

"Learn to be Happy" e Book on Smashwords.com now Draft2Digital.com

"Growth and Decline of the Economies of Europe and the US" e Book on Smashwords

"Homeopathy for Prevention of Diseases and Self Medication," e Book on Smashwords

"Be a Rational Pessimist: Hope for the Best, Prepare for the Worst," e Book on Smashword.com

"Defeating the Islamic State" e Book on Smashwords.com now Draft2Digital.com

"America Needs Donald Trump; Here is Why." E Book on Smashwords

"Grandpa's Tips on Navigating Through Life," self-published at Notion Press.com

"Grandpa's Tips on Management for All," self-published at Notionpress.com

"Ambush and Other Stories," self-published at Notionpress.com

"Keeping Fit with Homeopathy, Allopathy, Traditional Medicines, and Self-Medication,"

"Prevention of Diseases and Self-medication." Notionpres.com

"Prevention and Management of Stress," Notionpress.com

Bibliogrphy

The book has been researched from the internet. The sources of information have been mentioned next to the text. Terrain information and information about roads and bridges has been based on Google Maps. I have also used information provided in books written by me like "Outstanding Victories of the Indian Army," "Who is Afraid of the Chines Dragon: I am," and "The World Should Help Tibetans Liberate Tibet." No classified information has been accessed from any source.

Map 1

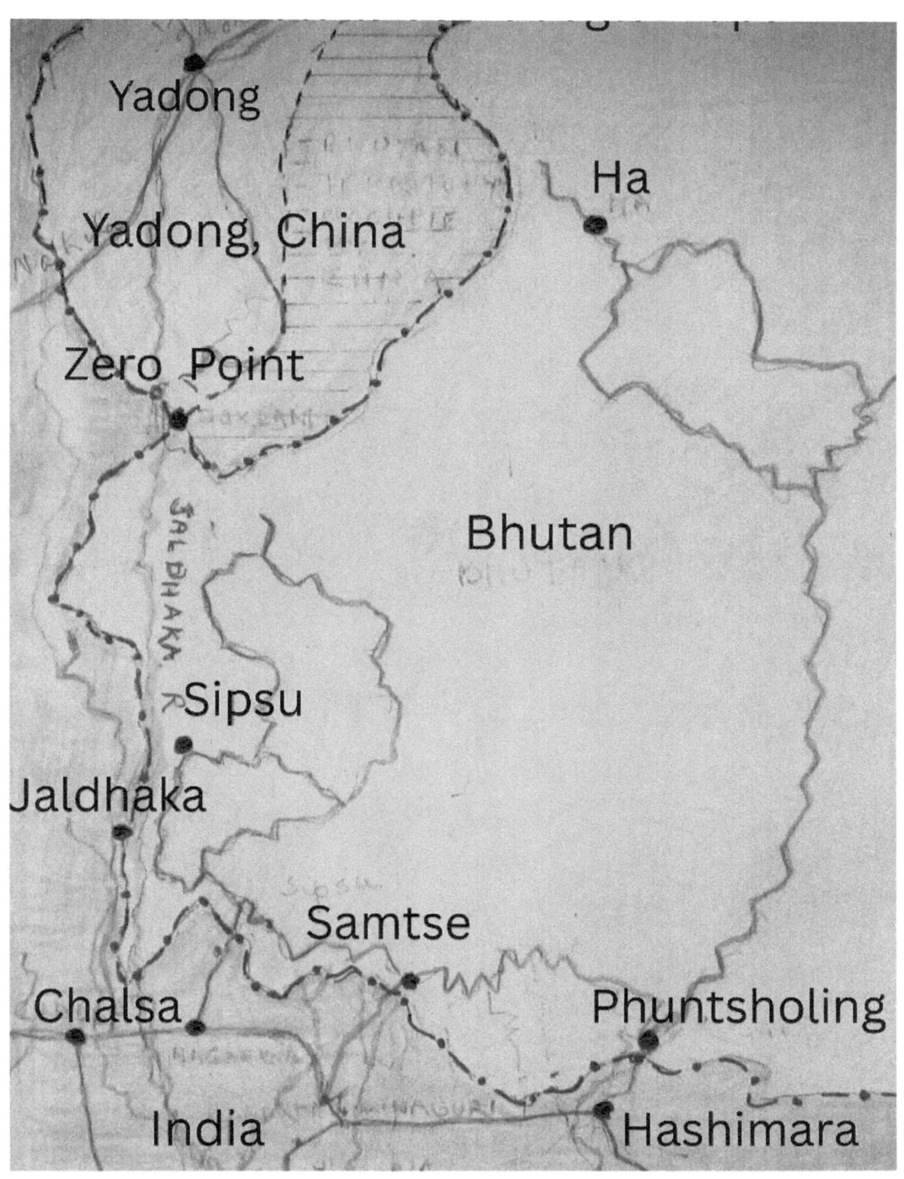

Map Of Yadong County and Samtse Bhutan

MAP 1

Map 2

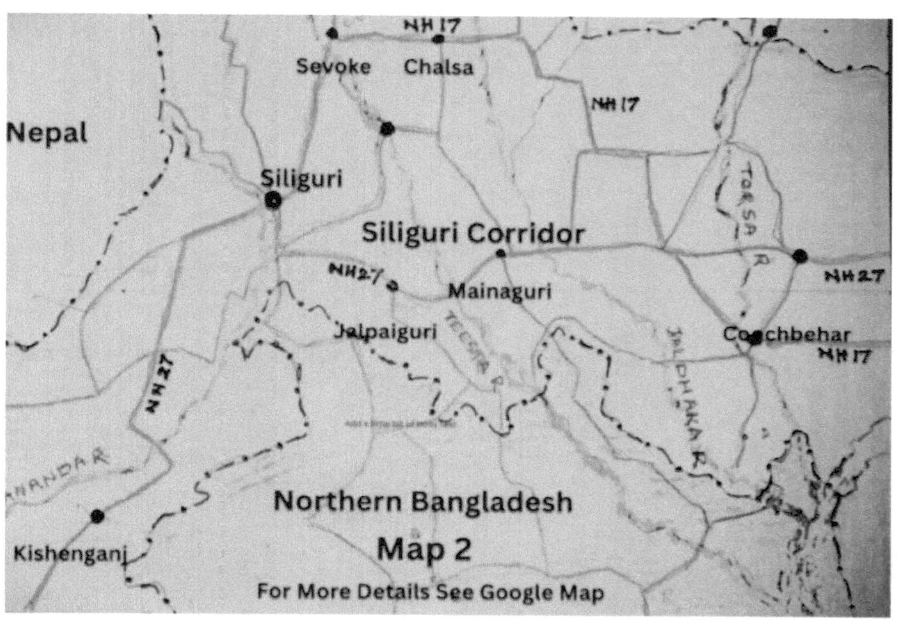

Shiliguri Corridor

Map 3

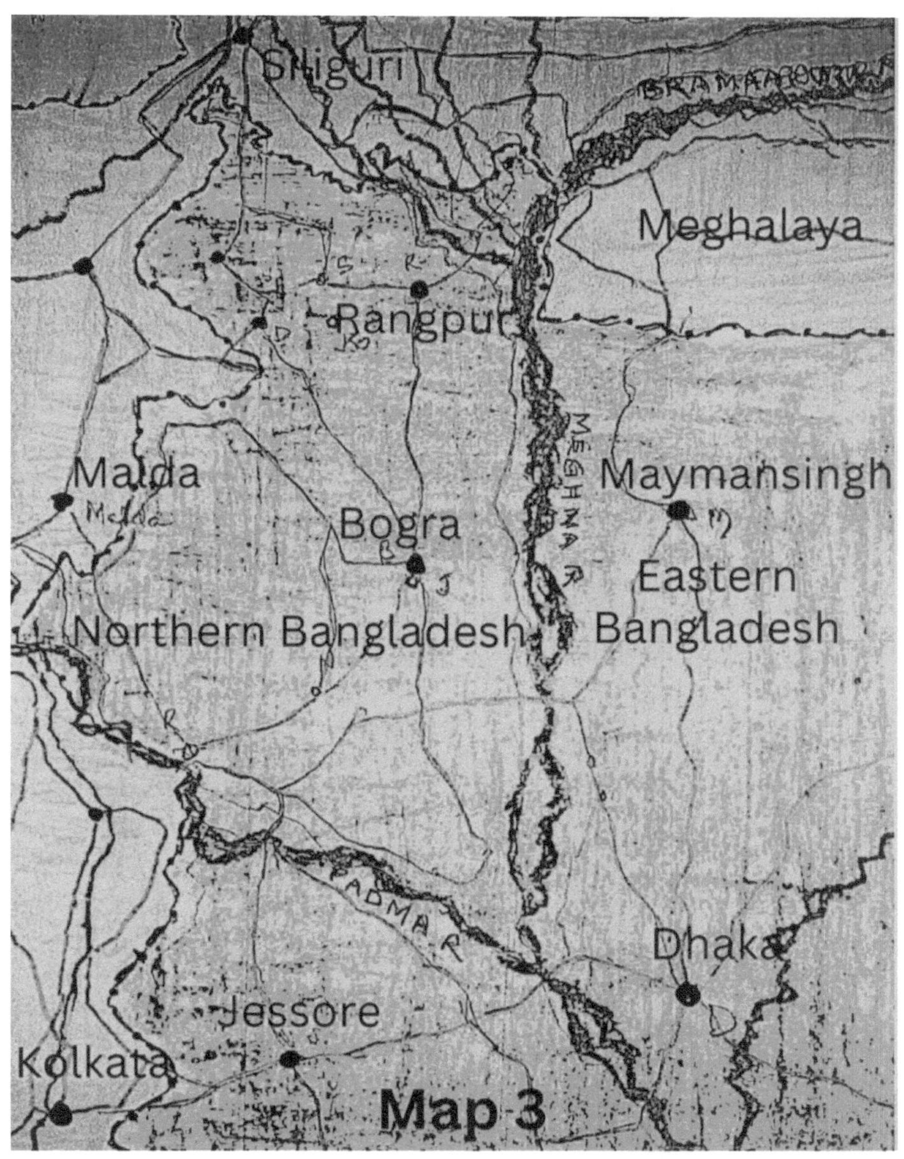

Map Of North Bangladesh

www.ingramcontent.com/pod-product-compliance
Lightning Source LLC
Chambersburg PA
CBHW062219150726
47991CB00006B/2342